Leo Maddox

LEO MADDOX

SARAH DARLINGTON

Thanks for reading!

Sarah Darlington

LEO MADDOX

Cover Design by Sommer Stein of Perfect Pear Creative Covers

This is a work of fiction. Names, characters, places, brands, and events portrayed in his book are either a product of the author's imagination or are used fictitiously. The author acknowledges the trademarked status and trademark owners of various products referenced throughout this work of fiction, which have been used without permission. The publication/use of these trademarks is not authorized, associated with, or sponsored by the trademark owners.

To all the fans of Leo Maddox. I wrote this especially for you.

CHAPTER 1:

I have a sick, twisted, fucked up mind. Hey, I'm Leo Maddox. All that comes with the territory. But I am who I am…and it's not really who I want to be. I've been trying to break free from my own personal stereotype my entire life. Nothing ever seems to change. But I've come to my breaking point. Either change or give up.

And I will never give up.

So here goes…

* * *

I woke up in a cold sweat, gasping for a decent breath. One brutal image played on repeat in my mind. The girl I loved—the girl I'd loved my entire life—with her plump little lips circling another man's…

Well, you get the idea.

And he wasn't just any man. In the dream, the man was her husband. Somehow that made this vision even more brutal for me. He was a dorky husband too. Glasses. *Not that there is anything wrong with glasses. On occasion I wear them myself.* Polo Shirt—that he still wore during their horrific love-making act. Silver Prius parked outside in their moderately sized driveway. *Why the Prius stood out in my mind? Who knows? Like I said, my mind can be a weird, strange place.*

And Clara was happy. She was happily married to this dorky sap from my dream. They were trying to get pregnant. She wanted to start a family. Meanwhile, my life was exactly the same—boring, repetitive, and painfully empty. Painfully lonely.

But I guess, on the bright side, I still had tons and tons of money.

Ugh. I crawled out of bed—distraught, angry, and sick to my stomach—and I stumbled across the penthouse room, my bare feet on hardwood floor. I despised this floor. Hardwood was for dining rooms and entry ways, not bedrooms. It pissed me off, as many random things always tended to do. I reached the bar cart, but, *fuck me*, it was empty. Of course it was empty. I never kept liquor in my room because I couldn't handle that sort of temptation. But in this moment, I regretted my personal *rule*. Well…maybe the 'no alcohol thing' was more of a personal *guideline*. Still, I never kept it where I slept.

I glanced out my window, scratching at an old scar on the underside of my arm. The shining lights of New York City were pretty damn amazing. Pouring myself a glass of water instead of the vodka I really craved, I stared at everything in miniature form. Looking at it all *almost* calmed me. Almost, but not really. The city was too fast paced and I always felt fast paced while here. I needed something slower before I snapped.

Reaching for my phone, I called my personal assistant, Regina.

It was late. (Or early?) But she answered after only one ring. "Morning, Mr. Maddox. What can I do for you?" her groggy but polite voice asked.

"I need the jet ready for Blue Creek."

"Blue Creek?" she repeated as if I'd told her I wanted her to go to Jupiter. "But the reopening is Sunday," she urged.

I didn't bother responding. Frankly, it bothered the shit out of me that she even questioned me. After a moment, she must have understood why she was getting silence and she muttered, "I'll make the arrangements, sir."

"Thanks. Call me when we can leave."

I clicked off my phone, tossing it on the bed. I needed to pack. *But what do you pack to impress a girl who fucking hates your entire existence?*

Suits. You pack suits.

CHAPTER 2:

Things move fast when you have money. Snap your fingers and people respond.

By the time I finished packing, the jet was fueled and ready. My driver sped Regina and I to JFK airport and the next thing I knew we were boarding my father's private plane—leaving New York City behind for Blue Creek, Virginia. Regina didn't usually come with me on my personal trips, but we were in a time crunch with the reopening happening in less than two days. I needed her with me as a way to kill two birds with one stone. This impromptu trip wasn't like me either. Work always came first. But after this morning's brutal yet enlightening dream, I realized that there were more important things than reopenings or my father's dreams. Or even my grandfather's dreams. My future was at stake. I could feel it in my bones. I *had* to be in Blue Creek tonight. I just had to be.

My driver's license said I belonged to New York. And I suppose if you took one look at me, you'd agree. I lived in upper class, upper Manhattan where standards were high and people's superiority complexes were even higher. That was my world. Well…that was my world ninety percent of the time. The other ten percent of the time I belonged to the little town of Blue Creek, Virginia. Blue Creek was a whole other planet, a lesser planet, but I loved it. I loved the fresh air, the slower pace of life, and the dewy smell of fresh cut grass on Reed Ryder's perfectly manicured golf course. As far as appearances and pretenses go, I was a Manhattanite through and through. But I ached when I was away from Blue Creek—probably because Blue Creek was my only tie to the girl I loved.

Growing up, I spent summers in Virginia and the rest of my time in NYC. Reed Ryder *(you know, that professional golfer famous in the late 90's)* was my father's best friend. Way back in the day, my father helped Reed start a little resort/country club in the middle-of-no-where, southern Virginia. Beautiful country. Beautiful golf club. But after my mom, the gold-digging bitch that she was, decided to abandon us, my father and I spent less and less time in Virginia and more and more time everywhere else.

These days, Blue Creek meant absolutely nothing to my father. In fact, he loathed the small town. He still cared for his best friend, but other than our annual Thanksgiving and Christmas dinner with the Ryder family in Blue Creek, my old man never went back. And then this past Christmas, for the first time ever, we spent our holiday in Southern France, far far away from the Ryder family.

It was the worst fucking Christmas on record.

So when my father put his Blue Creek house up for sale, ready to write off Blue Creek once and for all, I bought the house. It was ten-thousand square feet sitting unused on the edge of Reed's golf course and it was mine. Now all I needed to do was tear the place up and renovate.

The plane touched down, bringing my thoughts to the present. As we taxied across the small runaway, I considered how this evening might play out.

Reed was holding one of his parties. He always held plenty of these parties in his country club's ballroom. And I loathe them. Which didn't make much sense given the fact that I loved wearing a tailored, expensive-as-hell new suit. I loved the cusp between sober and drunk. I loved to dance. And I loved the Ryder family. Maybe my real problem with these parties wasn't actually the party, but instead the fact that it was always sheer torture watching Clara talking to and dancing with anyone but me.

So, my grand plan tonight was to ask Clara to dance. I never had before. It would be new territory for us, and because of our family ties, I knew she'd feel obligated to say yes. Then—while she had her arms wrapped tightly around me—I'd whisper something special to her. *I still need to figure out what that special something is.* She'd suddenly see me in a brand new light. She'd see the real Leo buried underneath my designer suits and pretenses, and fall madly in love. *Simple, right?*

Shit. Not simple.

My plan sucked.

I needed to come up with a better one between now and then. Maybe Maggie could help me.

My whole life I'd been best friends with Maggie Ryder. Reed had two daughters. Maggie and Clara. Identical twins. Well, identical in looks alone. Maggie was the good twin. The safe twin. She was polite and kind. And she was extremely easy to be friends with. That said a lot, since I was extremely difficult to be friends with. Maggie could handle my different moods, take my bullshit, and at the end of the day still make me laugh. How easy life would be if I could simply love Maggie instead of Clara?

But I couldn't. And I would never. Because I only saw Clara.

"What's our schedule going to be like?" Regina asked. She always needed a schedule and she always needed us to stay on it exactly. Suddenly, I regretted bringing her along with me. It would have been better to have her eyes and ears back in New York City. I guess my brain hadn't been functioning properly this morning when I insisted she come. Shit. Not to mention, my dad was going to have a stroke when he realized I'd just up and left.

I glanced at my watch. It was already almost noon. We'd lost half the day.

"I'll have the car drop me at Reed's house. You head on over to my place, get settled in the guest house, order us some lunch, and I'll be there in an hour so we can start breaking down the schedule for Sunday."

She didn't look happy at the prospect of us being separated for an hour. Regina was needy and work obsessed. But she said nothing and simply nodded.

When the car dropped me in front of Reed's house, I took the deepest breath of Virginia air that I could manage. *Would Clara be home right now? Was she even living with Reed this summer?* She, Maggie, and I were all the same age. I dropped out of college after my freshman year. But Maggie and Clara, both much better students than I, would have just finished their junior year at Virginia Tech. I knew that much, but not much more. I never asked about Clara because I was the only one who knew of my own personal, life-long, life-altering crush on the girl. I kept my feelings close to my heart and let no one else near that.

"Leonardo!" Reed roared when I knocked on the front door. He engulfed me in an immediate hug. "It's been months. You look taller."

"I feel like shit," I muttered into his shoulder as he held onto me a second longer. "I didn't sleep last night."

The thing about Reed was…he was incredibly easy to be honest with. He didn't judge or belittle the way my father did. He listened. "Is Leo Jr. working you too much?" he asked, concerned.

"Nah. I am working a lot, but it's all my own doing. I came today for a small break. I leave tomorrow."

He frowned. "I worry about you."

"I'm okay. Just tired today."

He gave me a look.

I returned his hard stare. "Seriously, I'm okay. I feel better just being here."

Reed might not have known about my feelings for his daughter, but he knew everything else about me. He knew because he cared. He noticed when everyone else ignored my behavior. "Good," he said, sighing. "That's really good to hear. And I'm glad you came here for a break. You're always welcome. Anyway, c'mon on in."

I followed him inside, shrugging out of my suit jacket. I dropped it by the front door. It was too damn hot for all my usual layers. "Is Maggie home?" I asked.

He shook his head no as we entered the kitchen. It smelled like something delicious was cooking in the oven. Reed was an amazing cook. Being a single father meant he'd had to learn how on his own years ago. But instead of learning how to cook only simple, basic meals—the man took cooking to the extreme. The same way he mastered everything he did, Reed was a master chef.

"You missed Maggie by about two minutes. She got all dressed up for tonight's party then left to get her hair done. She hasn't taken this new 'Clara and Andrew' development very well."

What.

The.

Fuck.

I cleared my throat. *Had I heard him correctly?*

"Did you just say Clara and Andrew? As in Andrew Wellington? Maggie's Andrew?"

Andrew Wellington, aka Shit for Brains, was Maggie's ex-boyfriend. I thought when they split up months ago, that was going to be the last time I'd ever have to hear his stupid name.

Motherfucking hell.

"Yes," Reed clarified. "Sorry, did you not know? I figured Maggie would have told you by now. Clara is dating Andrew. They started seeing each other about a week ago, but they've been inseparable since. Clara's bringing Andrew as her date this evening. And I have a feeling the shit's going to hit the fan tonight."

My heart plummeted to the floor. I was going to be sick.

No, the shit had already hit the fan. My nightmare had become reality.

CHAPTER 3:

Stay sober. That was my only thought as I entered the Reed Ryder Ballroom later that evening. To hell with doing work with Regina. Instead, I'd spent the last several hours getting ready and mentally preparing myself for this evening. I wore a sharp, light gray Armani suit with a white shirt, brown tie, brown belt, and brown Bottega Veneta shoes. Someone once told me that gray brought out my blue eyes. Not that I gave a damn about that sort of thing, but my eyes were usually the first thing women commented on so why not wear something to draw focus to them? Add in my perfectly styled black hair and I was at my best.

I looked the part. I felt the part. Even if I hated the part.

Clara, Maggie, and I had been born into this world destined to become friends. Mrs. Ryder and my mother used to be so close, closer than sisters, that they planned their pregnancies to coincide. The three of us kids shared birthdays, milestones, countless family vacations, summers in Blue Creek, and every holiday with the exception of this past Christmas. In addition to sharing so many good memories, we also shared one of the worst. Losing our mothers within a few days of each other. Mrs. Ryder died of cancer and my mom, so grief stricken by the death of her best friend, ran away. Or so goes the story I'd been told me entire life. The twins—then and now—were my family, my siblings, and my home. And as close as Maggie and I remained over the years, the opposite happened with Clara. I fell in love with her, not long after losing our mothers, and that was the first nail in Clara-Leo-friendship-coffin.

But hell if I was going to let her end up with an asshole like Andrew. Reed's information gave me new motivation. Tonight was more important than I'd originally thought. *So you have to stay sober!*

Drinking used to be my crutch. In social situations like this, I was very rarely seen without a martini or a beer in hand. But as shitty as I felt about Clara, I couldn't afford to lose control tonight. So I found Doug the cater-waiter, a guy I'd known for years, because I needed his help. We weren't friends, but for a hefty tip, Doug would do anything for me.

"Just bring me water in a martini glass please. Garnish it with an onion so it looks like a Gibson martini. Keep them coming as fast as I drink them." I slipped him a hundred dollar bill and he didn't question my strange request. It was one I had asked of him before. People expected me to drink, drinking was what these people did, and so I gave them the impression they wanted.

"Yes, sir," he replied and within minutes I had a water-martini in hand.

The night progressed. I watched Reed dance with every person in the room. The man knew how to have a good time and no matter the occasion, he was always the life of the party. Many of the people in the room came specifically for him. He had an infectious charisma about him. If thoughts of Clara dating that fucker weren't still lingering in my head, I might have enjoyed my time with Reed. The man served as a second father to me, maybe more of a father to me than my actual father, and he was one of the few people in this world I actually enjoyed being around.

Then suddenly I felt a woman's fingers slide over my shoulder. "Leonardo," a voice worse than screeching hyenas whispered in my ear. "It's been a long time."

"Leah. Hi."

A very beautiful, very surgically enhanced, woman in her mid-twenties wrapped her hands around my neck. I peeled her off me. She frowned playfully, trying her hardest to entice me. Leah Longerburger never gave up when she wanted something or someone. We used to mess around as teenagers, but I wasn't sixteen or desperately horny anymore. I didn't find things like her bleached hair and fake boobs so attractive these days.

"What is it?" I asked her. "Because I'm not in the mood."

"You're no fun anymore," she pouted. "Still pining away for Maggie Ryder? Now that Clara is dating Andrew you must be pretty thrilled. So, where is Maggie? Or is she too hurt by her sister to bother showing?"

"You're jealous," I told her. "I'm just trying to figure out of who. Maggie or Clara? Or is it both?"

"No. I'm just bored. Andrew Wellington was a lousy lay. Hell, all of the guys in this town are lousy lays. You weren't half-bad. Want to find out if that's still true?"

"Well, fuck me," I said, grabbing her gaze and holding it. "You just called yourself a slut and insulted me all in one breath. When you put it that way how could a guy refuse? Good night, Leah. Don't bug me about this again. It's getting pathetic."

Then, grabbing a fresh glass of martini-water from an approaching Doug, I sauntered away from the notorious Leah Longerburger. I only wished I would have had the same good sense at sixteen, when I lost my virginity to her on the grass next to the sand trap on the eleventh hole.

Claiming a seat at an empty table in the back of the room, I sat and rested my head on a dinner plate. *Leah and Andrew too?* I guess he hadn't waited long before moving on from Maggie. The news of him and Leah didn't necessarily surprise me. It just made Clara dating him all the more repulsive. What was going on with her? Was this some desperate cry for help? Maggie was the romantic one. The sister who fell in love often and easily. Not Clara. Clara was the take no shit and take no prisoners type. She lived the life she wanted and marched to the beat of her own drum. This news of her and Andrew didn't fit with her character and it had my head spinning.

* * *

Unaware of how much time had passed, lost in my thoughts and resting my head on my dinner plate, I sat up to Maggie hovering over me. *Finally, she shows!* She wore an elegant red dress and had her hair styled in precise waves. Even on her worst day, she never looked anything less than her best. She gave me a small frown, taking in my fake-inebriated state. I pretended to get fake-drunk all the time and Maggie never had the good sense to notice it as a hoax.

"Dammit, Maggie. Where have you been? I was beginning to think you'd ditched me," I snapped at her. My voice came out sharp, but all I felt as I looked up at my best friend was relief. Her breakup with Andrew 'the prick' Wellington happened months ago, but I knew a great deal of pain surely still lingered in Maggie's heart. And this news of Clara and Andrew being together... well, I feared it might have sent her over the edge again. But she looked okay. Better than okay. Completely composed. *Well, if she was okay then what took her so damn long to get here?*

Maggie pulled out the chair beside me and sat down. Her expression screamed of worry for me. "Do you need to get out of here? I'll go with you right now if you need me to."

I didn't answer and instead glanced upward at a very tall, very muscular, random dude standing behind her. He had tan skin and short brown hair. Where did he come from? Had he been standing there the whole time? Maggie had a date. A date I completely missed until just now.

“No, I'm fine,” I told her. “Totally peaches. I wouldn't want to disrupt your date.”

Rent-A-Date remained very still, assessing the situation and watching my interaction with Maggie. He reminded me of someone, maybe an actor, but my mind was having a hard time placing him. He wore a plain black suit, plain shirt, and plain tie. All very generic. *Where did Mags find this guy? The yellow pages? The side of the road?*

Being polite, Maggie introduced us. “Dean, this is Leo. Leo, this is Dean.”

“Dean,” I said in sharp voice, trying the name out on my tongue. It didn't seem to fit him. “Why don't you sit down? Save us from breaking our necks here.”

Guys like Dean never liked guys like me telling them what to do, but he sat anyway. Not beside Maggie, but in a random chair at the opposite end of the table. I stretched my hand out for him to shake and he returned the gesture without hesitation.

Something about Dean rubbed me the wrong way. Maybe he was harmless, but I decided I didn't care for him. Doug passed by the table at that precise moment and I signaled for another fake-drink. “Another Gibson, please,” I ordered, knowing that things were about to turn sour.

See, this was why I didn't drink. I didn't need alcohol to send me over the edge since it inevitably happened anyway. The blood under my skin boiled and the fight or flight instinct in my brain buzzed to life. Fight, I always chose fight. Dean hadn't done a single thing to me, but somehow I knew I couldn't trust him. Somehow I knew he was lying about something. Tomorrow Maggie would be pissed at me for ruining her date, but at least I could blame it on my fake-intoxication rather than admitting my shitty personality was at fault.

Both Dean and Maggie ordered a drink from Doug. Maggie opted for a glass of wine and Dean asked for a soda. And something in my brain finally clicked. I narrowed my eyes at Dean. I realized what was bothering me about him. I already knew him. But his name wasn't Dean.

“Have you seen Clara tonight?” Maggie asked.

“Negative,” I answered, keeping my eyes locked on this guy. He had some nerve coming here after all these years.

“So…she didn't even bother showing?”

“Thank the fucking Lord for that.” I was grateful now that Clara wasn’t here. She didn’t need to see me beat Robby Harvey’s ass into the ground.

Maggie saw the animosity growing inside me and she tried to distract me by making conversation. That wouldn't work. Not now. Not when I’d recognized Dean as Robby Harvey. And the bastard sat only feet away from us. My protective instincts kicked in. Did Mags even realize who she'd brought as her date?

Robby Harvey. Time had transformed him. Six years ago, when we both saw him last, he was much shorter and thinner, with long, hippie-style hair. He didn't have the bulk and muscle he had now. But even with all the changes, how could Maggie not recognize him? He used to be her step-brother! She used to date him! She almost lost her virginity to him!

“What was your name again?” I asked, my voice taking on a mocking tone. “Dan?”

“Dean,” he corrected.

“Funny. You don't look like a Dean.”

The waiter returned. He handed out our various drinks. I took a big swallow and then continued to push Robby. “Have we met before?” I didn't want to flat-out announce who he was. I wanted Maggie to recognize him for herself. *C'mon Mags, don't be so dense!* “You look very familiar,” I rattled on. “I'm positive I know you from somewhere.” Maggie still hadn't made the connection. I was losing patience fast. "Mags, where did you find this guy? He looks an awful lot like—"

"Clara and Andrew are here," she announced, cutting me off before I could spill the truth.

All thoughts of Robby Harvey were suddenly forgotten. I sucked in a sharp breath, while my eyes refocused across the room.

Clara.

She was actually here. She looked more beautiful than ever. She wore the sexiest, tightest fitting black dress I'd ever seen. It showed off all her perfect curves. Her long platinum hair had natural wave and I loved how she always wore it wild and free. As she moved closer, I noticed that she had pink streaks through her hair. *Holy shit.* I never found crazy colors in girls' hair to be attractive, but it looked positively sinful on her. Against my will, I felt all the blood in my body start rushing to the wrong spot. I shifted in my seat and instantly my fingers brushed over that same old scar on the underside of my arm.

Everyone said Maggie and Clara were identical, but to me they were nothing alike. They walked different, talked different, and made different facial expression...even their personalities were polar opposites. And while over the years Maggie and I grew to be best friends, the same never happened with Clara. It never happened because I was in love with her. I could function normal around Maggie. But around Clara I forgot how to breathe, how to be civil, how to act like a human.

Thanksgiving. That's the last time Clara and I had been around each other. And seeing her now made me realize how much I'd missed her. We didn't have any form of a relationship, but I missed her just the same. I wanted to start trying to make things right with her. I wanted to make tonight be the night that I changed destiny between Clara and I.

And then I noticed Andrew and all good intentions left me. My focus had been so zoned in on Clara that I hadn't initially noticed him standing with her. He had his arm synched around her waist like he was afraid that if he let go she might run away. He laughed at something she said as the pair moved through the crowd. They appeared to be walking in our direction. My desires faded fast and were replaced with anger. Maggie slid out of her chair and moved to an unoccupied one next to Robby.

"Um... Showtime," she whispered to him. "I think she's coming this way."

So did that explain Robby? Maggie brought him here to make Clara jealous? I'd all but forgotten about the crush both twins used to have on their ex-stepbrother bastard. My heart rate spiked and my fists clinched under the table. I didn't know who to hate more. Maggie for bringing Robby. Robby for being born. Andrew for having his hand wrapped around Clara's waist. Or Clara for being blind enough to fall for Andrew Wellington's bullshit. But I had to reevaluate that thought because I still don't think Maggie knew exactly who was sitting beside her.

"Calm down, Leo," Maggie said, noticing my rage. "You're too drunk to get in a fight with her. Let me do the talking. I promise I'll handle it."

Handle what? Nobody could *handle* Clara. It was one of those things I loved and hated about her. I shot Maggie a nasty look before finishing off the remainder of my water, wishing it wasn't water.

Clara paused at Maggie's side. She never once took any notice of me. Why would she? She really couldn't care less about me. She only saw her sister. Andrew on the other hand, with his beady little eyes, stared venomously at me. It creeped me the hell out. I tried to ignore him and instead studied Clara. Up close I noticed her hair had grass in it. *Had Clara been rolling around in grass?* A nasty image of her and Beady-Eyes having sex on the golf course popped into my head. I synched my eyes closed. *Kill me now.* But wait... Reed's mowers collected the grass clippings. Nobody could possibly get that much grass in their hair by sheer accident alone. My eyes flew open. Something didn't add up. Clara wasn't in love with Andrew. That's for damn sure. She just wanted to give the impression that she was. *Why?*

"Hi, Maggie," Clara said to her sister, her voice polite. Friendly, even. "How's it going?"

As if she hadn't noticed her sister's presence until just then, Maggie leaped out of her seat like she'd been probed in the ass. Her wine spilled in the process. Clumsy butterfingers tried to catch the glass before it fell to the floor, but she stumbled and almost fell into Robby's lap. The glass shattered and Maggie pretended not to notice. Was this her idea of *handling* things?

"Glad you decided to show," Maggie said. "Nice hair. Did you dye it with Kool-Aid?"

My stomach hit the floor. *Really, Mags?* Of all the insults, she comes up with Kool-Aid? I hated when she and Clara fought. But if she was going it do it, she might as well come up with better material.

Clara let out a bored sigh, the weak comment rolling off her thick skin. "Seriously?" she said. "Is that the best you can do? Kool-Aid. No, I found a five-year-old to color it with crayons. He gave me a good deal. Why, you want his number?"

"No," Maggie muttered. Her mouth opened, as if she had more to say, but she quickly closed it. *Poor, Mags.* She was drowning. Verbal warfare wasn't a talent of hers. And when she tried all she managed to do was look like a fool. Me on the other hand... I could *handle* these types of situations with ease.

So, despite all my big plans for this evening, I fell right into my usual behaviors. I jumped straight to Maggie's defense. Without hesitation, I got my ass out of my seat and moved around the table to face Clara.

"Clara." My voice came out strong and steady. And that trait of mine, the one my dad called a talent, reared its ugly head. "What Maggie's trying and failing to say…is that none of us are buying into your bullshit. You look calm and composed on the outside, but I know that's not how you really feel. You're starting to sweat. You're regretting letting Andrew stick his disgusting tongue down your throat, and all that grass in your hair didn't get there by accident. Whatever you're trying to prove, this isn't the way. I can see right through you—and so can everyone else." And then I added a plea I normally wouldn't. One that was more for my own sake than for Clara's. "Clara, please. Stop this."

The girl I'd known my whole life didn't even flinch at my words. In fact, they only seemed to bore her more.

"That's a little harsh, Maddox, even for you," Andrew told me through gritted teeth. "Do you even know where you're at? Why don't you crawl out of Maggie's ass, go find yourself some coffee, and mind your own damn business for once in your life." He rested one hand on my shoulder. "This isn't your concern, bro."

I saw red. I swatted Andrew's hand off my body. "It's more my concern than it will ever be yours," I barked at him. "And I'm not your *bro*."

"Leo," Maggie urged. "Stop it. He's not worth your time. People are watching."

"I don't care who watches. And yes, this is worth every bit of my time."

Appearing out of nowhere, Robby—whom I forgot existed for a moment—shoved his large body between Andrew and I. "I love a good show, but this isn't the place," he said. "If you guys are determined to make it happen, then let's go outside. I'll even play referee."

My anger refocused on Robby. I hated his face. I hated the way he'd left Maggie behind all those years ago. "This isn't your problem, Dan.

Now, *back off!*"

"Calm down, Maddox. I'm not your enemy."

"No way," Clara breathed. My words hadn't gotten a reaction out of her, but Robby's somehow did. She swallowed hard, daring a better peek up at him. Doing what Maggie couldn't, Clara noticed him for who he really was. It caused her face to turn stone-cold. Then she turned and marched out of the room without saying another word to anyone.

Andrew raced after her.

Dean visibly relaxed, but the tension inside me only doubled. "What are *you* doing here?" I spat at him, no longer willing to keep up with the charade. "You must have some brass balls. After all these years, I can't believe you dared show your face again. Do you have a death wish or are you just that stupid?"

"What's going on?" Maggie asked, still confused. "What are you talking about, Leo?"

Robby sighed. "Maggie sought me out, not the other way around," he told me. "I'm living in the area again and followed her here tonight for nostalgia purposes. But you're right, I shouldn't have come."

"Um, could someone fill me in here," Maggie begged. "Please? And Leo…stop looking at him like that."

"Mags," I scolded. "C'mon, you're smarter than your hair color. Okay then. I'll leave you two alone to figure this out. *Dean*, I'm sure you're just dying to reminisce about the good o' days, but after tonight, don't ever let me catch you here again. Not unless you want to find my fist in your face." I turned to Maggie to say one last thing. "Always."

And with that closing word, I left Maggie to figure this one out on her own.

CHAPTER 4:

Grass. There sure as hell wasn't grass like this in New York. I cut across Reed's golf course, ruining my shoes in the process, moving in the direction of my house. Driving home wasn't an option. My mind was too messed up for that right now. My hands shook and my heart raced. And for the life of me, I could not calm myself the fuck down. I couldn't even think about Maggie and *Dean*…because the words I'd just spoken to Clara replayed in my head like a bad dream.

I can see right through you. No, actually, I couldn't see through Clara. I was very good at reading people. But not Clara. Never Clara. And was it physically impossible for me to be nice to her? *Dammit.* Why did we always have to end every conversation in a fight?

Wanting to scream, wanting to shout, wanting to curse the world—I settled on an apology. My feet changed direction and started moving my body toward Clara's house. I had no excuses for my behavior. But I would apologize just the same. Clara might hate me for the rest of eternity, but at the very least I owed her an apology for all my asshole ways. Both past and present.

And then, as I was cutting through a predominantly wooded portion of the golf course, I heard a distant sound. Laughter, maybe? The noise sounded almost like Clara's laughter. I froze dead in my tracks, listening hard, wondering if my mind was playing tricks on me. Because for a moment, I only heard crickets and nothing else. Then suddenly I saw a golf cart racing in my direction. It was Clara behind the wheel—Clara and no Andrew.

Holy shit. She was coming at me fast.

There was only one option left. I could spend the rest of my life waiting, wishing, and hoping something would change between us. Or I could do something. *Would an apology win her over? Hell if I knew.* Probably not. I needed to do something drastic. So when her golf cart neared, I stepped out of the shadows and into her direct path.

Not my most brilliant moment.

I had not thought this one through. Because when the corner of that golf cart clipped my ass, it hurt like a motherfucker. Pain radiated down my leg and shot up my spine. The force of the impact knocked me through the air and face first into the grass. From the corner of my eyes, I watched Clara scream, swerve the golf cart, and come to a screeching halt beside my limp body.

"Are you okay? Are you okay?" she shouted, her voice filled with fear. I heard the soft sound of her feet stumbling through the grass and coming toward me. "Please don't die on me! I'm *so* sorry."

What? Was she genuinely worried for me?

I cursed under my breath. Because, even if she was concerned for me, I needed to play up the pain. I didn't want her knowing that I purposely stepped in front of her golf cart. *How crazy would that make me?*

I felt her standing beside me, my face still buried in grass.

"Leo?" she suddenly demanded. Gone was the anxiety in her voice. And now I understood everything. She hadn't known it was *me* she'd hit until this very moment. She'd been worried when she'd thought she'd hit some 'innocent' bystander. But me…hell, she loathed me so much that I was expendable.

"What the hell, Clara?!?" I barked, angry at her for not caring more. I deserved it, but it still hurt. I sat up, pressing my palms to my tender thigh. "You did this on purpose," I snapped, saying whatever I could to push the blame onto her. Shit. We had the most dysfunctional relationship on the planet. Why couldn't I ever break away from that?

"Yes," she said sarcastically, her blonde hair windblown and her mascara a little smeared. "I tracked you down and ran you over on purpose. Next time you'll think twice before saying anything nasty to me. No, of course I didn't do this on purpose!" She ended her sentence by suddenly kicking off her heels and kneeling next to me.

I froze, stunned.

Her bare legs were lost in the long grass. Her black dress hitched up high on her thighs. And for a small second I saw a glimpse of the black panties she had on underneath. I couldn't breathe. I couldn't think. I couldn't speak. *Why was she so fucking close to me?* Reaching for my hand, her fingers touched my skin. She attempted to peel my hand away from the leg that I was so desperately gripping. I didn't budge, but now we were touching and my eyes connected with hers. "Let me see what I did," she urged, her voice softer than it had been. Only once or twice before had I heard her voice soften like this. *Was it just for me that this sometimes happened?* That small change in her tone sent my blood pumping and my heart jackhammering.

For the briefest moment, I felt something between us. *Could she feel it too?*

No, I decided. This wasn't the first time I'd felt something spark between us only to have Clara ignore me or verbally jab at me in the very next moment.

"No thanks, I'm fine," I muttered, swallowing hard, and drawing away from her touch. I was nervous as hell and I didn't want her touching me. I wanted her to touch me because she wanted to touch me—not because I was hurt.

"Then you're going to have to take those off so I can see how bad it is." She meant my pants. "I need to know if we should call 911 or get you to a hospital." Suddenly, she reached for my belt, holding nothing back.

Holy shit! I jumped straight to my feet. "Whoa there, killer," I joked, forcing a laugh. "Let me buy you a drink before you take my pants off. Like I already said, I'm fine. You didn't hit me that hard."

She groaned, pissed at me all over again. Whatever moment there may or may not have been between us a second ago, was squashed in an instant. "I know how hard I hit you and you can't be fine."

I could show her fine. Testing out my leg, just to prove her wrong, I walked around in a full circle. Actually, my leg wasn't too bad. A little sore, but I'd live. "See? Fine," I said, patting my thigh. "Nothing's broken or bleeding. I'm going to have one hell of a bruise tomorrow, but other than that...I'm fine."

"Stop saying the word 'fine'," she groaned.

"Stop pestering me and I won't have to keep saying it," I replied.

From her knees, she let out a long sigh and glared up at me. "What were you doing out here in the first place?"

There was no way in hell I'd answer that question honestly. "I could ask you the same question," I reflected.

"I was going home." Brushing the grass off her knees, she climbed back to her feet and plucked her shoes from the grass.

"Well, I was going home too," I answered.

"Whatever." Again she sighed dramatically—as if talking to me was the most painful thing imaginable. But then she surprised me by saying, "C'mon, I'll give you a ride back to your house. It's the least I can do for running you over."

Instead of arguing, I simply followed her. I didn't want to fight anymore. I didn't want to say anything else that I would regret tomorrow. So I shut my mouth and climbed into the passenger seat of her golf cart.

She drove toward my house.

It was dead silent—nothing but us, the night sky, and the golf course. I rested my head on the back of the seat and enjoyed this small moment alone with her. The wind blew her hair around her shoulders and she drove on the cart path this time—no more joy-riding for her this evening.

Watching her drive…she was stunning. And, whether we were fighting or not, whenever I was with her, the bad stuff in life simply faded into the background. The man that someday would win her heart was going to be the luckiest man alive. I wished with all my being that that man could be me. Even fighting with her was better than spending time with anyone else. But I knew better. I had everything money could buy—but I would never have Clara.

I closed my eyes, suddenly too exhausted to keep them open.

And I must have drifted asleep because the next thing I knew the golf cart was stopping. "Leo. You're home," Clara informed me as she poked my ribs to wake me.

Struggling to return to consciousness—since it had been over twenty-four hours since I'd last slept—I rolled from my seat and proceeded to fall straight out of the golf cart onto the hard cement below. My bruised leg cramped up on me and I could barely move. Clara hurried around the golf cart and came to my aide. I tried to tell her to stop and that I could manage on my own—but instead of listening, she took my arm, placed it over her shoulders, and led me toward my house.

Dammit. Exhaustion was getting the better of me. I tried to speak again, but my tongue felt heavy in my mouth. Clara helped me inside and up the stairs toward my room. I dropped like a heavy rock onto my mattress. Then, with my face already pressed into my comforter, I let sleep sweep me away. Clara was leaving. This strange night was over. Maybe in another six months some other family function would push us together again. Maybe by then I could learn how to be civil, pull my head out of my ass, and control my temper around her. Maybe the stars would align and I could tell her how much I loved her.

Maybe.

But as my father had pressed into my skull at an early age, I knew maybe was only a synonym for no. And with that final thought, sleep hit me.

* * *

At some point, just before dawn, I woke up in a sweat and still in my suit. My head was ringing and my room was too damn hot. I still had on my shoes for fuck's sake. Stumbling out of bed, I stripped off all my clothing. I flung each piece of fabric across my room as I undressed—angry and annoyed.

What the hell was wrong with me?

I thought over the few moments I'd shared with Clara the night before. The least I could have done was to tell her goodbye. I hadn't even managed that. No wonder the girl hated me so much.

Naked as the day I was born, I padded across my room toward my open door. The spot on my thigh was a little tender but feeling better.

I'd live. Unfortunately.

I shut the door and stumbled back across my vast room. Clara must have left the door open and I didn't want Regina barging in on me in a few hours. She was out in the guest house, several yards away from the main house, but I expected her to come find me soon enough. She knew how to knock, so I didn't bother locking the door. Opening a window, I then crawled back on top of my bed, face buried deep in my pillow, and fell asleep all over again.

The next thing I knew it was light out and I heard Regina's voice. The noise came from the hall outside my bedroom door. Blinking the sleep from my eyes, I glanced across the room and saw the door ajar. "Hello, Miss Maggie," I heard Regina say.

Great. Apparently Maggie was here bright and early. And fuck, I was still naked.

"This is a surprise," Regina was saying to Maggie. *What was a surprise?* It didn't matter. I just wanted to get the hell out of Blue Creek.

Quickly, not wanting either woman to see me, I slipped out of my bed and moved for my dresser. I pulled on the first pair of jeans and t-shirt I could find. It was time for me to get back to New York. Time for me to get back to reality. My grand plan of wooing the girl I loved had failed miserably. Now the only thing I had waiting for me was Sunday's reopening.

"He's sleeping," came a whisper. "I've got to go."

Holy Mother of all things holy.

It wasn't Maggie speaking to Regina. That was Clara's voice out in the hallway. Regina had never met Clara before and she must have mistaken the twins. My heart jumped around in my chest. *Shit. Shit. Shit.* I walked for my slightly ajar door. *Who had opened it? Regina or Clara? Dammit, what was Clara doing in my house?*

"Nice seeing you," Clara told Regina. Her back was to me as I peeked through the crack in the door. I think she was pretending to be Maggie, trying to say whatever she could so she could escape before I woke up. *Well, this sure as hell was a surprise.*

"Regina, that's not Maggie," my mouth blurted out as I nudged the door open wider. My throat was dry from sleep and my words sounded scratchy, but I fucking loved that Clara was still in my house. "That's Clara. Could you please give us a minute?"

Like the good employee that she was, Regina smiled politely, nodded, and walked away. Clara stayed frozen with her back to me, clearly not expecting me to have woken up. But that didn't explain why she was here? She wore the same black dress she'd been in yesterday. Her hair was a tangled mess of blonde and pink. It was rumpled and sexy and had me slightly aroused. Then it occurred to me…Clara never left my house last night. She must have slept in one of the rooms. And just the thought of her sleeping in *my house* had my chest feeling all slippery inside. Breathing became difficult. *Was my door open because she'd been checking in on me? Was she concerned about my leg?*

Wait…had she seen my bare fucking ass too?

Oh, God.

After a moment, Clara turned around and faced me. Her cheeks flushed red. *Flushed!* I smiled, unable to hide my feelings. She had definitely seen my ass. And if I wasn't mistaken, I think she liked what she'd seen. She wouldn't be so red right now if she hadn't. Hell, she couldn't even look me directly in the eyes.

"What are you still doing here?" I asked, very amused and slightly annoyed. My whole life I'd been waiting for her to notice me. And instead of noticing *me*, she'd noticed my body. But then again, hell, at least she'd noticed *something* about me. Praise Jesus my gold-digging mother had been a *hot* gold-digging mother and I'd gotten all my good looks from her.

Clara looked everywhere except directly at me. "I stayed last night—in your Grandma Bunny's room, I think—just to make sure you weren't going to die or anything."

"Aww," I mocked, having too much fun with this. "Who knew you cared for me, killer? That's sweet."

"Well. Since you're alive and obviously *fine*," she groaned, growing instantly annoyed with me. "I'll just let myself out." She turned, ready to leave me.

"Clara, wait," I said, my voice coming out rather desperate. Vulnerable, even. I hated to let so much emotion show, but I couldn't let her leave. I just couldn't. Not like this. She glanced back at me, over her shoulder, and her gaze drifted up to meet my eyes—finally. She inhaled a sharp breath as her gray eyes connected with mine. Her cheeks flushed all over again and she made no more attempts to leave.

What. The. Fuck. Was I imagining her reacting to me?

My teenage years were a blur and I'd fucked a lot of faceless girls during that time. I was celibate now, but that was beside the point. Nevertheless, I knew…without doubt, then and now…that I had a certain *effect* on women. Clara had always been immune to my charms. So what the hell was happening now? I had to be imagining this.

Clara's face turned sheet white. No, I wasn't imagining anything. Clara felt this too and I could tell it was scaring the shit out of her.

Suddenly Regina returned, interrupting us and pissing me off. It made me want to fire her on the spot. I thought I'd made it clear I wanted her to leave us alone seconds ago.

"Mr. Maddox. Miss Clara. I don't mean to keep interrupting, but Mr. Maddox, you're way behind schedule. The plane was scheduled to leave at ten. Should I cancel the first meeting? We could try to postpone, but that might be tricky."

"What time is it?" I asked, peeling my eyes off Clara so I could glare at Regina.

"Almost eleven."

"Dammit. Okay then...don't cancel or postpone anything. Not yet.

Have Jeremy get ready to fly and I'll be downstairs in ten. Everything else is in order, I assume?"

"Yes, sir."

"Thanks, Regina," I said, ending our conversation. Regina disappeared down the hall, but I remained still. I watched Clara. I was so damn confused. "Want to go to New York with me?" I suddenly asked her, shocked by the boldness of my own words. But I had to try. I had to take this chance. Because I might not ever get another one.

Her jaw dropped a little. "What?"

My heart was racing, but I tried to play it off. I sighed, rubbing one hand over the back of my neck. Damn. I'd never been so nervous. I'd known Clara forever, but that didn't change the fact that my stomach was a mess. "You heard me," I told her, trying to talk in my usual fast way. "I'm leaving in ten minutes, so you can come or not. But I think you should come. You look like hell and I'll bet you could use the break and the distance from Blue Creek. We've recently refurbished the Maddox Hotel in Manhattan. The big reopening is this weekend. I have tons of work and won't have a minute of free time for myself. But if you wanted...you could fly up there in the jet with me, stay in one of the executive suites, do whatever, and then come back with me early Monday morning. Are you supposed to be working for your dad this weekend?"

Did I actually care if Reed needed her to work at his country club this weekend? No. Did I actually think she looked like hell? Shit, no. Of course not. She was stunning. But I still worried about her recent decision to date Ass-Face Andrew. Something felt off with that, and with her. Something made me want to keep her close—whether I benefited from it or not.

Yes, I loved her. Yes, I wanted to practice making babies and marry her one day…if I could only break down all her walls. But above all else, I cared for her. The Ryder family was my family. She was my family. So my question for her to come to New York wasn't completely selfish. That was the most shocking part of this conversation.

Because I was a very selfish person.

Clara hadn't answered. Maybe she was in shock. Maybe she was weighting the options in her mind, trying to decide. One thing I knew for certain, she needed space. She always needed space when faced with a decision or when she was put under pressure. It was part of her personality. I can remember when we were kids, she'd often disappear or run off to her room—especially after an argument—needing time alone. She'd reemerge stronger than ever. She never showed her true feelings to anyone. But I secretly knew, something I learned long ago, that Clara had the kindest, biggest, most gentle heart under her thorny exterior. It was part of why I loved her so much. I only hoped that if something were to finally start between us—if this moment was about to define the rest of my life—that she could learn to let me in.

I stepped backward into my room. "I need to take a quick shower. The car's in the driveway, waiting to take me to the local airstrip where my jet is. If you want to come, then be in that car in ten minutes. Bye, Clara."

I moved for my bathroom, but turned around to say one last thing.

"I think you should come."

Not waiting for a response, I shut myself in the bathroom.

CHAPTER 5:

Dazed and confused. That was me. Currently. Standing in my shower.

The water ran down my face as I heavily breathed in and out. I stopped doing drugs when I was nineteen, so I knew I hadn't just hallucinated Clara in my house.

"Calm the fuck down, Leo," I said aloud. "She's going to be in that car."

But I couldn't calm down and I didn't really want to. I'd waited most of my life to feel this way. To have a chance. To have hope.

But was my hope wasted?

My mind jumped to a memory of Clara from last summer. We hadn't seen much of each other this past year. And before this weekend, this incident was the last time we'd even spoken. And like always, one simple conversation between us had ended in hurtful words spoken.

Last summer I was only in Blue Creek for one week. I had vacation time off from work. Rather than spending my week in Paris or Rome or somewhere grand, I came to Blue Creek. I knew Clara would be home from college and I secretly hoped I would get the chance to talk to her. But in six out of seven days in Virginia, I had yet to even see her. So on day number seven, with nothing to lose, I took a chance and went to the country club pool. Maybe we'd randomly run into each other there. I'd already tried my luck everywhere else.

Much to my surprise, minutes after stopping by the pool, Clara entered. She came in through the women's locker room, her flip-flops slapping on the pavement. She paused when she noticed me resting in a lounge chair across the way. We were both alone. She didn't have to even acknowledge me. But she did. She started walking in my direction. I wasn't dressed to swim. I hadn't actually expected to find her here. And now she was coming toward me in her fucking swimsuit.

"Do not have a heart attack, Leo," I muttered under my breath. "Be cool."

She walked closer.

Yeah, I was going to have a heart attack. There was no controlling my racing heart.

"Clara," I said as she neared. Despite the way I felt on the inside, my voice remained calm.

"Leo," she said. "It's like eleventy-hundred degrees out here and you're fully dressed. Aren't you miserably hot?" Kicking off her flip-flops and spreading out her towel, she lay down uninvited beside me.

"I'm fine," I muttered, unable to think of anything better to say. Like I said, she was in her fucking swimsuit.

Thank God I had on sunglasses because I couldn't peel my eyes off her body, especially her thighs. She had killer thighs—firm, sexy, tanned. I wanted to see what those thighs looked like wrapped around my body while my cock was buried deep inside her. Jesus Christ. I didn't need to think such intimate thoughts about her. Not when there were children present. Not when she wasn't even mine to think about.

"Whatever," she groaned, picking up the book she'd brought with her. It had some half-naked couple on the front. They were kissing. This surprised me. If I had to guess, I would have thought Clara would be into

science fiction or vampires or some shit like that. Not romance.

An hour passed. We were both just lying there. At one point during that hour, out of the corner of my eye, I noticed Clara's breathing pick up some speed.

Holy Shit. She was reading something dirty. I knew it and I couldn't move or speak because of it. Something had turned her on and dammit if I wasn't half-jealous and fully-turned on now myself. This was the best hour of my entire seven day vacation. I closed my eyes and relished in this small moment, wondering desperately what she was reading.

"Why are you here?" Clara asked, cutting off my thoughts. "The pool in your backyard is better than this one."

My eyes flickered open. "Hmm?"

"You have a pool in your backyard."

"I'm aware."

"So, why are you here?"

"If you're so annoyed by my presence, you don't have to sit next to me. Nobody's breaking your arm." I wasn't exactly sure why she was pestering me with these questions all of a sudden. I couldn't tell her the real reason I was here.

"I'm not annoyed," she groaned. "I sat by you because I wanted to. Why can't we just get along? And I do really want to know...why this pool?"

I took a deep breath. Did she really want to 'get along?' Because right now it sure felt like the opposite. "Relentless, aren't you?" I grumbled.

"Are you gay, Leo?" she suddenly asked.

What.

The.

Fuck.

Was that the vibe she got when she looked at me? Women were constantly coming on to me. Why didn't I affect her in the same way? I stood to my feet, yanking off my sunglasses so I could see her better. "Do you spend your free time just trying to think of ways to purposely piss me the fuck off, Clara? Because you're really good at it and it's working out too well for you."

She followed me to her feet. Her hands landed on her hips. "No," she said softly. "If you're gay, you can tell me. I wouldn't tell anyone else."

"I want to know why you're asking me this," I said through gritted teeth.

"I don't know," she huffed. Her chest rising and falling quickly. "You always dress so well—better than girls—and you have such a weird friendship with Maggie. I've never seen you with a girl or even heard Maggie mention you dating someone. Don't be such a homophobe, it was an honest question."

"First, you assume I'm gay and now you accuse me of being a homophobe. Which is it, Clara?" I groaned. I might love her, but right this moment I'd never been more pissed at her. "I have a question for you. Are you gay?"

She blinked up at me. "What?"

"Where's your boyfriend? Where are all of your girl friends? I haven't seen you with either. You certainly excelled at being a tomboy growing up. And even now, even when you go to the pool—" I glanced deliberately down at her one-piece swimsuit. It looked like something she'd bought from Goodwill. It was beautiful on her because she was beautiful. But something nicer wouldn't have killed her. "You can't dress for shit. So why don't you satisfy my curiosity...are you a lesbian? If you are, you can tell me. I wouldn't tell anyone else."

She yawned. She actually yawned! And she started acting as if talking to me was the most boring thing imaginable. Her eyes were cold as she said one last thing to me. "Grow up." Then she dropped to sit and fell back down onto her towel.

"We will never get along," I groaned, glaring down at her. "Because you will never stop infuriating me. If you must know, I came to the pool today because I wanted some company—or at least the illusion of it—but I'd prefer being alone to being with you."

"You're blocking my sun," she replied, indifferent.

I groaned again, even louder this time. "You're insufferable. I hope your milky-white skin burns. And buy a bikini. You aren't eighty or fat, so I don't get why you're always wearing that damn thing."

She let out a slow, bored breath. "This suit used to be my mother's, asshole. Now can you please move? You really are blocking my light."

For once in my life words failed me. I couldn't win with Clara. No wonder she hated me. When we fought, I always ended up saying something nasty, something I couldn't take back. I walked away, wishing everything could be different between us.

I scrubbed my skin under scalding water, scrubbing off that memory. Then I very quickly towel dried, picked out a fresh suit, and got ready. Not bothering with my bags because I wasn't sure when I'd be back here again, I hurried downstairs. By the time I was locking the front door, it had been almost twenty minutes since Regina told me the time. I skipped down the stone front steps, heading straight for the waiting car in my driveway. My heart was in my throat and one thing was on my mind.

Would Clara be in that car?

By all means, she had every right in the world *not* to be. I fully expected her *not* to be. I yanked open the door and slipped inside. And my heart expanded.

She was there. She was *fucking* there.

We didn't even make eye contact as I settled into my seat. No words were exchanged. Regina told the driver we could leave and the car started to move. On the outside—I was my normal calm, slightly detached self. On the inside—my heart was wild, raging, screaming. Regina started talking business on the drive to the airport. I listened. I responded. I played the part I was born to play. But my heart was with the girl sitting across from me in the rumpled black dress. Words couldn't describe how happy I was that she had come with me. Even if she ignored me all weekend long…this meant something.

Two hours later the plane landed at JFK airport. I noticed I had five missed calls from Maggie. But rather than calling her back now, I stepped off the airplane and into the black town car that would take us all to the Maddox International Hotel and Tower on the Upper West Side. Maybe I would call Maggie later. But she didn't know about my infatuation with Clara and I really wasn't ready to explain why I'd brought her sister along with me to New York.

The car carried us closer to the hotel. Regina continued to go over everything for tomorrow's reopening. My dad wanted me to be versatile within the company. So over the past few years, he'd bounced me around from job to job. Working everywhere from housekeeping (*had that really been necessary?*) to managerial jobs. I was putting in my 'dues' as he called it. And after tomorrow's reopening went smoothly, I'd move up the ladder to something better.

But what Regina didn't seem to understand, as she went on and on, was I'd been living in my father's hotels my entire life. I knew the procedures. I knew how to walk the walk and talk the talk. I opened my mouth and the right words always came tumbling out. Charisma. My grandfather, Leonardo Maddox Senior, invented the word. My father inherited the skill. And I, Leo Maddox III, hadn't fallen far from the same apple tree. I had charisma in spades. Maybe I couldn't function properly around Clara, but I could put on a good show for everyone else.

As we neared the hotel, Regina ran out of things to discuss. We all rode along in a comfortable silence. With nothing else to do, I watched Clara. It was a safe moment to do so because her eyes were wide and staring out her window. It was if she'd never seen the tall buildings in the city before. Maggie came to visit me in New York about monthly. But maybe it had been longer since Clara had been here. It made me wonder where her head was at.

"What are you thinking?" I asked, the words escaping me before I could stop them.

She looked at me, seeming surprised I'd spoken to her at all. "That I'm glad I came," she answered.

"Good," I responded.

In the next second, thankfully before things had a chance to get awkward, the car came to a halt outside the grand entrance to the Maddox hotel. The very second we stopped, Clara leaped from her seat and out the door. Someone was waiting for her on the street—a tall brunette in a flowery dress. Stephany. I had met her maybe twice before. She was Clara's friend from Virginia Tech and she caught the girl in an immediate hug. Clara must have called or texted Stephany to meet her here. I hadn't known she knew anyone in the city but this was good…right?

It hadn't occurred to me before this moment, but what was I really expecting having Clara come here with me. That we'd walk hand-in-hand through Times Square kissing and taking photos? Of course she knew someone else in the city. Of course she had plans. I was still thankful she'd come, but this new development made my weekend suddenly seem much bleaker.

"Regina," I whispered. "Please get Clara checked into a room on the penthouse floor. The executive suite on the west corner is nice. She's my guest. Make sure she has everything she needs. After you show her to her room, come find me. We have work to do."

Regina nodded, always eager to do whatever I asked. She stepped out of the car, while I stayed seated for a moment. I watched Regina speak to Clara and her friend. Then the girls disappeared into the building.

"Dammit," I said aloud, burying my face in my hands.

* * *

Hours passed. Work kept me so busy today that I skipped lunch. And by seven in the evening, when I hadn't eaten all day, I was famished. I needed to take a break or I was going to pass the hell out. Taking the elevator up to the penthouse floor, I walked toward Clara's suite. I wanted to invite her to eat—as friends, at the very least. I'd brought her to New York. That meant it was my responsibility to make sure she had everything she needed.

But when I knocked on her door, there was no answer. I knocked again. Nothing.

"Hey, Shelly," I said, stopping a maid who was vacuuming on the other end of the hallway. "Have you see the girl staying in that room?" I pointed back to Clara's door. The maids were the eyes and ears of this hotel. I knew because I used to be one.

Shelly clicked off her vacuum and shook her head. "No. My shift started at noon, honey. No one has left or entered that room since I've been here. In fact, you're the only other person I've seen on this floor all day. Is something wrong?"

"Everything's fine," I told her. "Just wanted to check on the girl that's staying here this weekend. She's a friend."

"Okay, dear," she said. "I can let you know if I see her."

"Thanks, Shelly."

She nodded and then continued vacuuming the carpet that was already immaculately clean.

I walked away. But now I had an unsettled feeling in the pit of my stomach. It wasn't because I was hungry either. New York City could be a dangerous place. Clara was smart but also very impulsive. "Dammit, Clara," I cursed out loud, nervous as hell now.

There was only one thing I could do. I had to call her.

She was a big girl—she could do whatever the hell she wanted, but I needed to know she was okay. My heart raced and my stomach rolled as I pulled my phone out of my pocket, staring at it. I had her phone number. I'd always had her phone number. I'd just never used it before. It was only a phone call. I don't know why this was making me so nervous. I hit the button and made the call.

It rang and rang. Then rang some more.

"Jesus Christ, pick up your phone," I mumbled under my breath.

Just then, at the last second, she answered. "Hello?" came her voice, muffled. Wherever she was, there was a hell of a lot of background noise there with her.

"Hey Clara," I said, trying to act casual. "It's Leo. What's up?"

'What's up?' That's the best you can come up with? Pathetic.

"Not much," she answered.

"I just wanted to call to make sure you were okay. You're okay, right?" I was speaking a little too fast.

"I'm fine."

Hell, now I felt like an idiot for calling. She sounded perfectly intact. She sounded like she was off somewhere have a great time and I was the jackass interrupting. "Well, if you need anything, call or text me. Okay?"

"Okay," she answered.

And that was the end of our phone call. We both hung up at the same time—me feeling like a royal ass for even calling at all. But then, not one second later, my phone buzzed in my hand. It was Clara calling back. *Holy shit! She's calling you back. Answer it, idiot.*

I clicked to answer.

"Leo," she said, her voice so much more direct and sure than it had been a moment ago. "I'm in Brooklyn at this place called the Alligator Lounge. Steph works here and I'm just hanging out while she works. I know you said you were going to be busy and I'm sure Brooklyn is hardly your style, but if you're bored and want to—"

Wait. What? "Are you trying to invite me to come hang out?" I interrupted, my voice barely above a whisper.

"Yes," she said softly back, "I guess I am."

Several long moments passed. I was in total shock. Clara and I had never done anything *alone* before. Was she inviting me to come join her out of some sort of obligation or because she sincerely wanted my company? Then I realized…Clara never did *anything* out of obligation. She did exactly what she wanted when she wanted. She was constantly getting in trouble with her father because of it too. This was a real, honest to God invitation.

Holy shit.

"Okay then," I told her. "I'll be there in an hour or so." Pressing the button to end our phone call, not wanting her to change her mind or anything, I let out a long sigh.

This was it.

For better or worse—tonight was going to be the night I told Clara how I felt.

CHAPTER 6:

I stepped inside the Alligator Lounge. It was a bar. Small, intimate, and it smelled of pizza and beer. Music thumped and my heart pounded in a heavy rhythm to match. My nerves were shot and I wasn't sure how I was going to hide that tonight. I'd had to ditch Regina to make it here in time.

But I was here.

I'd chosen casual clothes—not my usual style. If I was trying to impress anyone else, I would have worn one of my suits. But Clara wasn't anyone else. The usual things didn't impress her. And I felt a little uncomfortable not dressed in my typical armor. Not a single person around me even noticed my presence. So, actually, my clothes situation—maybe it wasn't such a bad change.

I choose an empty seat at the end of the bar, my eyes scanning the room for Clara's blonde hair. So far I couldn't find her. *Shit. What if her invitation was some kind of cruel joke?* My stomach flip-flopped and my breathing wasn't quite right.

"Yeah, that seat's taken," the bartender said to me, approaching and patting his palm at the bar top. "Find another."

I glared at him. The place wasn't very busy and there were plenty of other empty seats around me. "I'll have a Sam Adams Summer Ale, please," I ordered, ignoring his comment.

He walked away, not acknowledging my order.

What an asshole.

Suddenly I felt a small tap on my shoulder. I turned around and found Clara standing behind me. She'd dyed her hair purple. Like lavender purple. And I fucking loved it. It fit her. But I wasn't really looking at her hair. With me sitting and Clara standing, we were exactly eye level. "Oh, there you are," I muttered, feeling a whole mixture of emotions. She was here. She was safe. She was more gorgeous in this moment than ever before.

Neither of us spoke, but I couldn't peel my eyes off her. The strangest part of all, she seemed to be having a similar problem. It was like…for the first time in her entire life, she was noticing me. Not just the suit, or my money, or my hair, or my smile—I think she was noticing something else. Whatever it was, it helped me start to relax some.

Well…until the bartender returned and rapped his knuckles against the bar top, much harder this second time. My small moment with Clara evaporated. "What did I tell you, dude? That seat's taken," the guy said.

Again, what an asshole.

"It looks unoccupied to me," I said, my voice nowhere near its usual calm and composed nature. "Why don't you do your job, stop bugging me about my seat, and get me the drink I ordered….do I have to ask you twice?"

The bartender leaned over the counter, glaring at me. "If you don't lose the attitude and stop harassing the other customers, then I'm going to have to ask you to leave."

"I'm not harassing anyone," I said through clenched teeth.

"The pretty girl standing right next to you? That's her seat you're sitting in. Move now or I'm going to come over there and move your ass for you."

My ass instantly moved out of the seat. Not for him, but for Clara. "I didn't mean to steal your seat," I said in one breath, having to pass awfully close to Clara as I moved.

Rolling her eyes at me, she sat down. But then she did something incredibly shocking—she smiled. "Do you have to pick a fight every night of the week?"

Staring down at her, I almost laughed. What was going on with us? We were actually getting along. "No, Sunday's are my day off," I joked.

The bartender lingered. *What the hell was his problem?* "Oh, you're here with her?" he commented. "Sorry, man. I just never would have put the two of you together."

"What that hell is that supposed to mean?" I demanded, wanting to kick his ass all over again. For the first time in my life I had time alone with Clara—this random asshole was stealing it all.

"Looks can be deceiving," Clara commented. Were her words meant for me or him? I didn't have time to decide because then she said, "I saw some empty tables in the back. Come with me."

Like I would turn down that request? Without a single thought, I nodded and then followed her deeper into the bar. We entered a mostly empty room with a pool table. Clara, even though she was wearing a leather jacket, shivered as the air conditioning was stronger back here. If I'd worn a suit, I could have helped her, but as it happened, I only had on a t-shirt.

She sat down at a table. Knowing I needed some distance, I sat in the chair across from her. For a moment I studied her. I mean *really* studied her. Between her purple, long wavy hair and the studded leather jacket she wore—she was seriously badass. In a rock star fantasy kind of way. Like something out of one of my wildest dreams. And despite the cool temperature of the room, my body was burning up.

"So," I said, clearing my throat. I reached out, fingering a strand of her hair for a second before pulling my hand back. I couldn't resist. I had to touch her hair. "Purple…interesting."

"Fine, let's hear it," she groaned. She flipped that long hair over her shoulder and crossed her arms over her chest. "Whatever carefully constructed cut-down you have for me, just say it now and get it over with."

Did she truly expect so little from me? I needed to start changing her opinion. Immediately. "I don't have anything to say. Not this time."

Her arms unfolded. "Well, that's a first."

Just then Clara's friend Stephany approached the table. I sat back in my seat. Was this how tonight was going to go? Everyone interrupting us? But I decided right then and there that it didn't matter. Even having the asshole bartender bother us—none of it mattered. All that mattered was that I was here with Clara. So that already made this better than any other damn day in my life.

Stephany had a full tray of drinks, which she balanced on her shoulder. She smiled eagerly at me—like she was excited to see me. *What had Clara told her about me?* I smiled politely back at the girl.

"Leo, this is Stephany," Clara said, introducing her friend. "Steph, Leonardo Mad—"

"Leonardo is my grandfather's name," I interrupted, realizing Clara thought I didn't know Stephany. "Nobody calls me Leonardo. Besides, I've already met Stephany….twice. Once, freshman year. And she came with you to the Masters Tournament, April before last. Your memory worries me."

"No," Clara argued. "You didn't even go with us to the Masters that year." Realization came to her face. Yes, I'd been at the Masters Tournament this past year. Yes, she was remembering me there. Honestly,

I swear. Reed was like family to me too. Of course I would have been there supporting him.

"Okay," she decided. "Maybe you were at the Masters. But when did you meet freshman year?"

It hurt a little that Clara could have forgotten this moment in our past. It was the moment I gave up cigarettes, gave up screwing random women, gave up my excessive drinking, and all around started to change my life for the better. "We ran into each other at an apartment party in The Village," I said, completely forgetting about Stephany standing next to us. I needed Clara to remember this. "You must remember. I certainly haven't forgotten the time I nearly fell to my death."

She remembered. I could see it her eyes.

The night I was speaking of happened two and half years ago. It was January and our freshman year of college. After a fan-fucking-tastic phone conversation with my father earlier that day, where he basically demanded I quit school and start working for him, I'd spent the rest of the day getting positively fucked up. I was so shitty that I could barely remember my own name. Somehow I'd ended up at a random party, sitting alone in the cold, on the railing of a balcony.

So many damn stars. I stared up at the night sky, with a bunch of hateful thoughts floating around in my head, and took a slow drag of a borrowed cigarette—borrowed because I'd been trying to quit smoking, but had once again given up after about twelve hours. I wanted out of this cycle. Out of my life. Would anything ever get better? I had so much to be grateful for, and yet, I felt so empty. Always empty.

"That's crazy disgusting even for you, Leo," came a familiar voice out of nowhere. "I'm sure you can think of more creative ways to kill yourself!"

"Clara?" As if divine intervention had magically conjured her, there

was Clara standing in front of me. The girl I'd loved my entire childhood. So damn adorable and snarky, just like she'd always been. She wore a barely-there halter-top that clung to her sweaty skin. Her light blonde hair stuck in little places to her neck, like she'd been dancing all night. She shivered as the cool air touched her skin but her eyes never left me.

"Shit!" I lost my concentration, dropped my cigarette, and fell backwards off the railing I'd been sitting on. My head hit cement and the hot end of the cigarette singed the skin of my forearm.

Clara rushed up to me.

"Dammit, gravity," I mumbled, half-joking half-serious.

Clara giggled. She actually fucking giggled. It was shocking. She hadn't showed me much emotion one way or the other for a very long time. And then even more surprising, she offered a hand to help me stand. "You dumbass," she joked as she pulled me to my feet. I think she might have been a little drunk. It was a Saturday night in a college town, after all, so this shouldn't have surprised me. But I'd never seen her like this before and it was cute.

"You smartass," I retaliated, smiling, and toppling into her.

"You must have hit your head pretty hard. I haven't seen you smile in years."

I pressed my lips together, trying unsuccessfully to wipe the smile off my face. Clara only laughed again. "Steph," she said, turning to her friend who I suddenly noticed standing with us. "Could you go inside and see if maybe they have some ice? He might have a concussion."

"Are his pupils dilated?" her friend asked. "I read once that's a sign of a concussion."

Clara stared directly up at me for a moment. Her eyes were wide and clear. All I could do was look down at her. "They are," she answered, not looking away from my eyes.

The rest of that evening was a blur. I couldn't remember leaving Clara. I couldn't remember how I made it back to my dorm room. But I couldn't forget the way her eyes had stared up at me or the hope I'd felt for the first time in years. Clara sat with me for a long time, most of that time a blur as well, making sure I didn't have a concussion.

When I woke up the day after, I felt changed. I'd hit a turning point, similar to the way I'd woken up yesterday morning. On that day, two and half years ago, I swore off drugs and random women. I created a set of 'rules' to follow when drinking alcohol. I quit smoking cigarettes cold turkey. I called my dad and made a choice—I gave up school and started working for him.

And I did all of it for Clara.

I did it all in anticipation of this moment. The moment she'd start to notice me. I wanted her to like the man sitting in front of her when she finally opened her eyes to what had always been in front of her. I wanted to be worthy. I'd come a long way since that night two and half years ago. And I still had a long way to go.

"I have no clue what you're talking about," Clara said, playing ignorant. But now I *knew* she remembered. "I went to lots of parties in The Village freshman year—they're all a blur."

A smile came to my lips. This was a fun game we were playing. "Don't lie, I know you remember. But this does make for an odd coincidence. I've now had two near-death experiences because of you. Last night—when you nearly turned me into road kill. And falling off that balcony. Do I need to watch my back around you, killer, or am I just that accident prone?"

The most adorable, shocked smile came to Clara's lips. "You're probably just an alcoholic."

"Or maybe I'm going to have to look into hiring a bodyguard." All of a sudden, I remembered her friend still stood waiting on us. As much as I liked playing around with Clara, we were being rude not including her in our conversation. “Anyway, nice to *officially* meet you, Stephany,” I told her.

Stephany smiled politely. “You too. I've got to go deliver these drinks. Want me to bring you guys back anything?”

Clara and I both ordered a beer and then Stephany left us. I took this moment, where we were getting along and actually talking, to tell Clara a few things I’d been waiting a long time to say.

“I haven't had a cigarette since that night,” I explained. “I have a little scar from where I burned myself in the process of falling on my face.” I turned my right hand over, exposing the underside of my wrist. There was a small white scar on my skin, barely noticeable but there. It was a scar I cherished. I traced the spot with my thumb. Clara, surprising the hell out of me, reached across the table and gently swept her fingers over the same area. She must have done this unconsciously because a second later she pulled away. My eyes jumped to meet hers. Her cheeks were slightly flushed and her breathing a little heavier than it ought to have been.

“Every time I get the urge to smoke—which is all the time—I look down at that scar and think of that night,” I told her. “And of you. I wish all my vices could be helped so easily.”

“And until the bruise on your leg heals, maybe you can look down at it and be reminded that you shouldn't walk through a golf course at night while you’re drunk. You never know when a crazy girl on a golf cart might hit you.”

“I'm kind of glad some crazy girl hit me. I wouldn't be with her now if she hadn't.”

Stephany returned right then to drop off our drinks. Shocked I’d been bold enough to say that, I picked up my beer and took a sip. Across from me, Clara did the same. Stephany lingered for a small second and then disappeared.

My eyes were still on the girl across the table. Her cheeks grew redder yet. She swallowed down several gulps of her beer, before finally setting it down on the table. It looked as if she was about ready to leap across the table and throttle me. Or perhaps…something…*nicer*. Her eyes screamed with a mixture of confusion, panic, and possibly lust. She was realizing there was something between us. She just *had* to be. And it was about damn time, too.

"What is it?" I whispered, my heart now slamming inside my chest. "Clara? Are you okay?"

"Why did you come here tonight?" she suddenly demanded. "We're not friends. You hate me."

I set down my beer, staring at the little bubbles that floated peacefully to the liquid's surface, and thought for a moment about how to answer. I needed to say the right thing.

"If I hated you, I wouldn't be here now," I told her.

"So why are you?"

"I could ask you the same question."

She rested her elbows on the table and leaned closer, her eyebrows raising. "You used that line on me last night. It won't work for you a second time. Tell me, Leo, right now. Why are you here?"

Again, it hurt that she thought so little of me. I was here because I loved her. It felt so obvious to me. "Why do you think I'm here?" I demanded, my voice coming out harsher than I wanted it to. "Why do you think I invited you to New York? Why do you think I almost got into a fight with Andrew 'Fuckhead' Wellington last night? Why do you think I still spend every summer in Blue Creek? Maggie isn't the only thing keeping me there. Why do you think I was walking in the direction of your house last night?" I ran my fingers roughly through my hair, not even trying to control my emotions anymore. “No. You know what? I won't answer your question, but I will ask you one of my own. Why did it take you *seeing me naked this morning* for you to finally start noticing me?”

Her mouth dropped open and she stared at me. Minutes passed and still she said nothing. I’d shocked her into silence. Now she knew *everything*. I’d just inadvertently told her *everything*. My feelings were on the table and I needed her to say something. Anything.

Suddenly she found her voice. “I saw you naked this morning and so-freaking-what if I happened to like what I saw, okay?” she snapped. “Are you trying to say you *like* me?”

“Yes,” I answered.

“No...No! NO! You can't. Not now. Not after all these years of being so mean to me. It's not fair. If that's how you feel, then why are you such a jackass?”

I took a very deep breath. Suddenly, a whole lot of shit made sense to me. Clara had a million and one walls built up and maybe, just maybe, she’d built them all against me. “You're right. I've been mean to you for far too fucking long. It ends tonight.” Then very slowly, very carefully, so she wouldn’t see how badly my hands were trembling, I slid my beer and hers to the other side of the table. I didn’t want anything to spill for what was about to come next.

“What are you doing?” she asked, her voice uneven.

I stood, not responding to her question, and started moving around the table. Clara caught onto what I had in mind because the next words out of her mouth were, “Don't you dare.”

Still I moved toward her.

“Leo,” she whispered in one final half-attempt to stop me. But the thing was…I could see it in the way her eyes were devouring me whole, in the way her cute little mouth dropped open, and in the quick fall and rise of her chest…there was no chance in hell she truly wanted me to stop. That gave me all the confidence I needed. I wasn't going to stop.

I took her small hand in mine and gently pulled. She stood to her feet and put up no fight as I caught her in my arms. That icy stone wall around her—it thawed and crumbled in an instant. Her eyes were big and wide, terrified and excited. Reaching up, I tangled my hands into her pretty purple hair and drew her closer.

I'd been waiting my whole life for this moment.

"I like you," I whispered close to her ear. "I more than like you. As hard as I try, I can't seem to stop and I sure as hell don't want to try anymore."

"You do?" she asked softly, tenderly moving her head in reaction to the touch of my fingers.

"Yes, I do."

My hand trailed from her hair to her face. I traced the curve of her jaw and then her lip with my thumb, memorizing. God, she was beyond gorgeous and her skin was even softer than it looked. I couldn't believe she was letting me touch her, letting me hold her, letting me be near her. I didn't deserve this moment. I'd never be worthy of this girl, but fuck if I didn't want her just the same.

"Clara," I whispered and brought my mouth down against her soft pink lips.

I'd fantasized about kissing her about a million times throughout my life. About where it would happen. About the way Clara might taste and feel. About her reaction. About my reaction. About the things I would say and do. But all of my fantasies instantly paled in comparison to the real thing.

I was done. I was sold. I was hers.

She smelled so sweet. After taking a moment to explore her lips, I slipped my tongue inside her mouth and found that she tasted even sweeter. Clara let out a small moan and pressed closer against me. She stood on her tiptoes, reached up, and wrapped her hands around my neck. *Fuck me.* As we kissed, her fingers dug into my shirt and trailed over my shoulders. She was exploring. She was touching. She was enjoying this. Meanwhile, I was so hard it was ridiculous and way too wildly inappropriate for such a public place. But I couldn't bring myself to care. Clara certainly didn't seem to care.

"You're amazing," I gasped against her mouth. "You have no idea how bad I want you."

Clara wobbled a little.

"I've got you," I whispered. My hands moved to the small of her waist and I lifted her up onto the table's edge. I was feeling bold with her now. Kissing her had shattered all the stone-barriers that had always held us apart. No longer self-conscious, no longer calculating my every move, no longer fearful every word out of my mouth would piss her off—I finally was able to let go. I nudged her thighs apart and moved in closer. Clara let me. She even locked her legs around my waist.

But suddenly I ripped my lips from Clara's and took one giant step backward. My movement surprised her because she gasped. I'd surprised myself as well. But I needed out of her grasp. I needed away. This was too much, too fast. And if I didn't stop myself right this second, then I wasn't sure I'd ever be able to stop. I had to stop. For my own mental wellbeing, I just had to.

My chest rose and fell as I stared across the space between us. I guess, at least for a moment, even after our kiss ended, it still felt like I was right there with her across the room.

"Ahem," came a voice. It was Stephany. "Thanks for the show, guys. I'm officially depressed, jealous, and missing my ex-boyfriend now."

Clara broke eye contact and looked to her friend.

Shit. Shit. Shit.

I could see it. The fear growing on Clara's face. This thing that just happened between us—it was the best damn thing that had ever happened to me. But Clara only looked horrified now. Stephany, seeing exactly what I was seeing, rushed up to Clara. She took her friend's hand in her hand. "We'll be right back, Leo," she yelled over her shoulder as she dragged Clara away from me—across the bar and into the ladies' bathroom at the other end.

I melted inside.

I sat back down in my chair, scared to death Clara would come out of the bathroom hating me even more than she did when this day began. But you know what, I decided—what the fuck ever. After years of wishing and hoping, tonight was the first time I'd actually done something. Anything was better than nothing. And if Clara hated me for the rest of her life for kissing her and bringing out something in her she wasn't prepared for, then at least I would always have that one kiss. That one moment with her. And there would be no more lies. I wouldn't have to cover up my feelings with meanness ever again.

Several minutes passed.

Dammit, what was she doing in that bathroom? Talking about me, I imagined.

Finally she returned. She seemed recharged somehow. Calm. Collected. Unaffected. She approached the table I hadn't moved an inch away from. I stood immediately. Instantly, I was a worried, nervous mess. I just couldn't cover up my emotions with her anymore. Not after what just happened.

Clara, the badass that she was, took her beer in her hand. Casually, as if I wasn't even there, she took a long sip.

"Are you okay?" I asked carefully.

Clara pulled the beer away from her lips. Then very unladylike, she wiped her mouth with the back of her hand and let out a big gasp of air.

"Clara?" I demanded. "What's going on? Say something, please. Are you okay?"

"Am I okay?" she asked, sarcastically, looking at me finally. *Shit, she was mad.* "What's that annoying code word you and Maggie used to say all the time? The two of you probably thought I was too dumb to crack that little language you created to use against me. Oh yeah, I remember now. Peaches. I'm just totally peaches."

Standing tall, she reached her arm and her beer high above my head. Slowly, she poured the remaining contents of her drink down over my head. I gasped, frozen, shocked, but mostly hurt. "Real mature, Clara," I groaned. By the time she was finished with her little temper tantrum, my hair, clothes, and face were all coated in liquid.

"That's for making me care," she told me, setting her empty glass back down on the table. And if my beer shower wasn't bad enough, she drew her hand back and slapped me across the face. Shit, it stung. She was much stronger than her small size suggested. I could have caught her hand and stopped her. But frankly, what was the fucking point anymore? "That's for being a jerk to me since we were kids," she muttered. Surprisingly, her voice wasn't as harsh as her hand had felt across my face. "And this..." She stood taller, grabbed hold of my face, and planted one firm kiss on my wet lips. "That's so you know I'm not fucking around." She continued to hold me tight, pressing a little closer into me. I was so damn confused, I couldn't move a muscle. "Prove it to me," she whispered, her voice shaky and raw and vulnerable as hell. "Prove to me you aren't an ass and I'm all yours."

Then she pulled away, rushing off—leaving the bar and me.

What the hell just happened?

CHAPTER 7:

“Wow,” I said aloud, debating. *Should I chase after Clara right now?* I knew how she was. I knew how she often needed space to breathe and think. This was one of those moments, but every bone in my body wanted to chase her. It was getting late. Where the hell was she going? Back to the hotel?

“Don’t chase her,” Stephany said. I’d forgotten her existence, but she’d been right there this whole time. “Trust me and don’t chase her.”

“I know,” I answered, tugging my hands through my wet hair, shaking off some of the liquid. “I know how she is. I know how she needs her space.”

“Oh.” Stephany stared big brown eyes at me. She was tall and almost my height. “You really like her, don’t you?”

I simply nodded. No point in denying it now.

“Then you should know, she took the key to my apartment. That’s where she went.”

My jaw dropped. “It’s ten fucking thirty! Is she going to walk?”

So much for not chasing after the girl. I hurried through the bar, racing outside. No chance in hell was I about to let her walk home alone. I had to catch up to her. I had to make sure she made it back to Stephany’s place in one piece.

Stephany chased me outside, into the street. "No, Leo," she urged, tugging on my arm. "My apartment is two blocks over. I walk it every night. It's safe. She's fine."

Dammit, this girl was strong. She had such a firm grip, but I was stronger. We played a ridiculous game of tug-of-war as I started off in one direction. "Stop being an ass," she moaned. "That's not even the right direction. Let me text her. She's probably already home."

I felt like a fool. But my heart and head were both spinning. I'd just kissed Clara. It hadn't been a fantasy this time, it had been a reality. I'd kissed her then she'd dumped beer on my head and told me to *prove it to her*. To prove my feelings. To prove I wasn't the asshole she thought I was.

"There," Stephany said, her fingers moving fast over her phone. "I texted her. She texted back. She says she's home. You happy now?"

"Yes," I muttered. "Thank you." *Why is she staying there and not at my hotel?*

"I need to get back inside before I lose my job."

I nodded, unsure of what the hell to do with myself now.

Stephany disappeared inside.

I walked. I walked until my feet hurt and I had to call my driver to come pick me up.

***

The next morning was the reopening. It went off without a hitch. A few of my father's celebrity friends even showed up, checking into the hotel, showing their support. I never understood how my old man had so many friends. They say money can't buy everything, but it damn sure nearly could. It couldn't be his winning personality that brought people in, could it?

Either way, my thoughts weren't on work today. They were on the girl with purple hair in Brooklyn. I wondered if she thought of me when she woke up. If she thought of our kiss. If she regretted the moment we'd shared. I needed to see her today. I needed to know if she hated me or if I had a genuine shot—

"Mr. Maddox, sir, I have a phone call for you."

"What?" I blinked several times, the vast lobby of the hotel coming back in focus. I'd zoned out there for a moment.

"Yes. It's a women on the line," one of the hotel managers explained. His voice shook as he spoke. I think this was the first time he'd ever spoken to me. Was I *that* intimidating? "She says her name is Detective Agent Ryder from the NYPD, but I'm positive she isn't a real police agent."

"Oh," I said, an involuntary smile spreading across my lips. It was Clara. "Maybe she was afraid you wouldn't put me on the line unless she lied. I'll take the phone. It's my friend."

He handed the phone my way. And then suddenly it occurred to me. *Why the hell hadn't she just called my cell?*

"Hello? Clara?" I said, my voice desperate, but I hardly cared. "What are you doing calling this line? Is something wrong?"

"Yes!" shouted back a voice. But it wasn't Clara's naturally calm and steady voice. It was a slightly higher pitched voice. "And this is Maggie, not Clara. Why would you automatically assume Clara was calling?"

"Because who else would come up with Detective Agent Ryder?" I joked, disappointed *and* relived that it wasn't Clara calling.

Maggie laughed then grew serious again. "How come you haven't been answering my phone calls? And what's going on with you and Clara? I know she ran you over with a golf cart."

I sighed. Here we go. I guess everyone now knew about Clara being here with me in New York. "I'm fine," I said. "I just have a bruise the size of Texas on my ass."

"Maybe you deserved it. I also just found out you're both in New York. How do you explain that?"

"Wow, Detective Agent Ryder, impressive skills of deduction," I groaned, hating how she was questioning me. I never questioned all her stupid life decisions—like dating Andrew Asshole Wellington for four years of her life. That's nearly a quarter of her existence wasted away on that fool. "Did you figure all that out on your own?"

"Leo," she urged, softly. "Stop, please."

"I'm not trying to be mean," I explained. "I haven't been answering your phone calls because this is exactly what I was afraid of—the voice of reason. Yes, Clara is in New York. I invited her and she came. For the first time in my life, she doesn't completely hate me." I stopped speaking for a moment and took a deep breath. No use hiding anymore. "This is probably going to come as a shock, but I have a thing for Clara. I have for a long time now. I've been afraid to talk to you about it because I know you'll bring me back down to reality and tell me how stupid I'm being for getting my hopes up over this. I'm scared shitless, but I don't want to come back down to reality, Maggie."

I swear to God, a good five minutes ticked by. Me waiting to hear Maggie's response. And Maggie saying absolutely nothing. Finally I had to say, "Maggie? Are you still there?"

"I'm here," she answered. "This is good, Leo. Really good."

What? Maybe I should have confided in her years ago. "You mean that?"

"Yes," she rushed to answer. "I think it's very good. All I want is for you to be happy. This...this is good. Clara still sucks as a sister and I can't stand all the dumb stuff she's constantly doing. I mean, really, who dyes their hair lavender?"

"It's pretty damn sexy," I muttered. "You'll hate it, but I love it."

"Ew, la, la, la," Maggie groaned. "We better set some ground rules before this goes any further." I laughed and then Maggie actually thought up some rules on the spot. "Rule number one, no talking about anything physical because I don't ever want to hear about that. Rule number two, you have to keep our friendship one hundred and ten percent separate from anything that happens between you and her. No matter what. Number three, if Clara and I get in fights—like you know we will—you always have to pick her side. Her side will be the irrational, moronic side and secretly you'll agree with me, but I'll be the bigger person and forgive you in advance for siding with her."

Unable to control it, an even deeper laugh escaped my throat. "I can't believe you're okay with this," I said, playing with the cord on the phone. "I thought you were going to freak the fuck out on me."

Maggie giggled for another moment then recovered. "I do want to say one 'voice of reason' thing. Just one. It's about Clara and Andrew…is she still with him?"

Oh holy hell. There it was. Reality. I'd kissed Clara and deluded myself into believing she was all mine. She wasn't. She had Andrew chasing after her too. "I honestly don't know," I muttered. Nothing was funny now. "I got a little worked up Friday night because I thought maybe Andrew might mean something to her. But when I saw her with him, I could tell she despised him as much as the rest of us. Which really makes me wonder—what the hell was the show for?"

Maggie huffed a breath into the phone. "Probably just to hurt me."

"Don't be so judgmental—not yet. Let me ask her about it and see what she says before you start World War III. Although, I'll have to admit, I was more thrown by her reaction to seeing Robby."

"How so?"

"Just that he got a reaction out of her at all. I know you both had a crush on him back in the day, and—"

"Don't, Leo," Maggie groaned. "Don't start that. You are your own worst enemy. That was ages ago and she went with you to New York, didn't she? That has to mean something. You're perfect, Leo. You're sweet and kind and she'd be lucky to have you. Just let her in—let her finally see the real you."

What if I'd already shown her the real me and that's who she hated? "The real me is what I'm afraid of," I told her with a groan. "But about Robby or Dean or whoever the fuck that was on Friday...when I get home, we'll get to the bottom of this. I promise."

"That won't be necessary. I don't plan on ever seeing Robby again."

"We could only hope, but doesn't it seem odd that the jackass randomly shows up after six years? And with a whole new name? Nobody just randomly shows up in Blue Creek. And nobody changes their name unless they have something to hide. Something's up, Mags. And as soon as I get home on Monday, I'm going to figure out what it is and put an end to it."

"Okay," Maggie answered simply. "But Leo, don't you ever ignore my phone calls again. No matter what. Remember? You and me against the world. *Always*."

"Always. But I'm tired of fighting the world, Mags. I'll see you on Monday."

"Monday," she repeated.

I hung up the phone, my stomach a mess. Was I worried about Robby being back in Blue Creek? Yes, definitely. He'd been a part of Maggie's life—of all our lives—for three short months over six years ago. Reed married Robby's mother, Monica, spur of the moment, and the pair only lasted for that small moment in time. Essentially, it had ended as fast as it started.

Surprisingly though, those three months had been really good months. Days spent bonding, playing golf, swimming, rafting down Blue Creek—Robby had befriended all of us, not just Maggie. But then Reed caught Maggie and Robby in bed together, seconds away from Robby taking her virginity. And that ended everything. Reed demanded both Monica and Robby leave immediately.

So, with barely even a moment to pack up their things, they both left.

And for as smitten as I'd thought Robby was with Maggie, neither of us ever heard from him again. Months slipped by, while Maggie continued to have faith. She believed, so wholeheartedly, that he loved her and he'd come back for her. He'd promised her he'd return one day. But he never did.

Until now.

So whatever his motivation was for coming home—I knew none of them were honorable. He was about six years past honorable and no better in my eyes than his gold-digging mother. Thank God he'd never set his sights on Clara the first time around. I hated what he'd done to Maggie, but I might have killed him if he'd harmed Clara the same way.

Clara.

Dammit, I needed to see her again today. With this reopening, it was the worst possible timing, but I needed to make something happen. And I would. I had a plan.

CHAPTER 8:

Yankees tickets. I loaded them into the box, along with two Derek Jeter jerseys—hell, everyone loved Jeter—and two foam fingers.

"Chicks love opening shit. Dude, you're a genius."

Paul Kage hovered over my shoulder. The two tickets I'd placed inside the box were his two tickets. Aside from work, and of course the Reed family, Paul and his family were my only friends. They were a rag-tag bunch of brothers originally from Staten Island. Their parents died when they were younger and the brothers meant everything to each other. And about six months ago, I met Paul in the bathroom of some dingy-ass bar.

It was on the night of my twenty-first birthday. I'd been alone and feeling sorry for myself. My father hadn't remembered the day and I'd decided to celebrate alone. Yet, all I really accomplished was passing out in some random bathroom in some random bar. Even after all the improvements I'd made since the night on the balcony with Clara—on occasion I still relapsed, still had nights where I drank way more than any one person should. Paul had been at the same bar as me that night. When I was too inebriated to function, he'd saved my ass from waking up alone and in my own vomit—something that had kind of become my birthday ritual.

Instead I woke up on his couch.

He hadn't known what to do with me, so he'd taken me back to his place. He'd taken care of me as I'd spent most of the night throwing up in his toilet. He even insisted I shower and borrow some of his clothes the next morning. It had been a strange experience for me—because most of the people in my life weren't anywhere near as kind as he was. And Paul had wanted nothing in return. Just doing his 'good Samaritan duty,' he'd told me. But I'd been grateful, and frankly…touched. To repay the favor, I'd purchased him, as well as the three brothers he lived with, season tickets to the Yankees. No big deal. It's not like I didn't have the means or the money to get him the tickets.

But the weirdest part of the entire experience—in the end, I'd decided to purchase myself a season ticket too. I liked Paul. I even liked his outspoken brothers. I wanted an excuse to hang out with them again. *Did that make me just as bad as my father? Had I bought my friends in this instance?* I wasn't exactly sure. But, as it happened, I'd grown close with the guys since that night.

When work didn't interfere, I never missed a game. So today, when I didn't have a clue what to do for Clara, I called Paul. I asked for his advice and he surprised me by rushing over to the hotel.

"Let me read the note you wrote," Paul nodded to the paper in my hand. "Trust me. I get more ass than a toilet seat. I'll tell you if it's good or not."

I chuckled. "You have a girlfriend. You liar."

"I'm not a liar. I get to have sex with her every night—which is much more than you can say. So give me the note."

"Fine," I groaned, feeling strangely protective of my note. But I handed it over anyway.

Slowly, his dark eyes scanned down the sheet of paper. After way too many seconds, he finally said something. "It's okay. I guess. Direct. To the point. Do you mean to sound so…*indifferent*?"

I swiped the note from his hands and reread it.

Clara and Stephany-

There's a Yankees game today at 1:05. Want to meet me there? Text me yes or no and I'll send a car to pick you up. If you already have plans, I understand.

Leo

Taking a deep breath, I decided that I *did* mean to sound indifferent. Last night I'd come on pretty strong and I didn't want to make the same mistake today. That was the whole reason I was inviting Stephany too. "Yeah," I said aloud. "Clara is… Clara's different than most girls. I don't want to scare her off. I just want to hang out with her."

He nodded. "Then I think you're golden. But after the game is over, if all goes well, then you should ask her to go out to eat with you or some shit like that."

Jesus. A date? Alone? Now *that* had my hands shaking.

"Anyway," Paul said. "I've got to go. I'll tell Tony and Charlie what's up. They'll be on their best behavior for you later at the game."

"Thanks again for the tickets," I told him. "I appreciate it more than you know."

"Nah, without you, I wouldn't even have the tickets in the first place. I don't mind missing one game in the name of love."

I laughed as I walked with him across the lobby. We said goodbye and then all there was left to do was have my box of baseball stuff delivered to Stephany's apartment in Brooklyn.

* * *

Clara never responded to my note. *What the hell?* After losing my cell phone for a couple hours and then finally finding it, I unlocked the home screen like a kid on Christmas. But I was sorely disappointed when I found that I had zero missed calls or texts from Clara. She'd completely ignored me. *Couldn't she at least have texted me a simple 'no thanks?'* I even tried calling her, just to make sure everything was okay, but my call went straight to her voicemail. So after that wonderful kick straight to the balls—I didn't know what to do with myself. But I wanted to get as far away from work as possible, so I decided to still go to the game.

But the game was pure fucking torture.

Paul and Richard weren't there. That left me with Tony and Charlie—the younger and more rowdy of the four brothers. And I just wasn't feeling social enough for them today. They laughed and joked like it was any other day, but I couldn't seem to shake the disappointment off my shoulders.

That kiss with Clara had been amazing. Even if I hadn't wanted her since I was six, it still would have been amazing. The way my body had fit against hers. The way my heart had felt like it might explode right out of my chest. I had expected a good kiss out of her, of course. But that kiss…that kiss had been something extraordinary—the stuff of fucking gods. *Did she feel nothing I had felt? My whole life, and especially last night, was I beyond delusional for wanting her like I did?*

"Dammit, guys," I suddenly voiced to the others and to two empty seats. "I need to get back to work before my dad realizes I'm missing." I stood from my seat, not really worried about my father, but wanting an excuse to get the hell out of here.

Tony groaned. "That blows that she didn't show. Sorry, Leo."

I shrugged like it was no big deal. But it was a big deal. "It is what it is," I told him. "I'll be out of town for at least tomorrow's game. Want me to send my ticket your way?"

"Sure." Tony smiled. "I've got this cute little honey I'd love to bring on Monday."

“Okay then. Later,” I told Tony and Charlie, putting on a smile but feeling like shit.

Then I left, marching up the stairs, ready to call it a day and to head home to lick my wounds. That was when I ran straight into an orange shirt.

And amazing purple hair.

Clara.

“You're here,” I stated, baffled but happy. She wore an orange shirt that I think a toddler might have scribbled on. Her purple hair fell in wavy locks around her shoulders. Her eyes were tired and her face frowning—but hell I was just happy she was here. My stressful day instantly became a whole lot less stressful.

“Of course I'm here,” she grunted, her gray eyes squinting out at the baseball field rather than making direct eye contact with mine. “I said I was coming, didn’t I? No thanks to you, by the way. We waited and waited for that car you said you would send, but it never came,” she rambled, speaking faster and faster as she went. “Then we were forced to take a taxi. I'm surprised we even made it at all. What the hell! Where are you going anyway? Are you leaving already?”

“Whoa,” I told her. “Slow down, killer. What?”

“Hi, Leo,” Steph said. I hadn’t even noticed her. Yet again. But suddenly she was there beside me. “Thanks for inviting me.”

“Hey, Steph,” I said back to her. “No problem. I'm glad you both came.” I shifted my focus back to Clara. “I told you to text and let me know what you were doing. When I never heard from you, I tried calling. Your phone was off so I assumed that meant you didn't want to hear from me. I should have sent the car—I would have, had I known you wanted to come. I should have sent it either way.”

“I texted you. *Then* my phone died. But I did text you.”

“Who cares, guys?” Steph interrupted. “Let's just go watch the game.”

She turned and moved in the direction I'd come from a few moments ago, toward the waiting seats, but I didn't follow after her.

And neither did Clara.

I moved a step closer, forcing her to actually look at me. Yes, we'd kissed. So fucking what. The least she could do was look at me. "Clara," I murmured. "Did you mean what you said yesterday?"

She swallowed hard, her eyes finally latching onto mine. At the contact, her pretty cheeks went pink. And suddenly I knew she meant it and my body started humming at the realization.

"I said a lot of things yesterday," she whispered, deflecting. "It's hard to remember."

I frowned. Dammit. I thought when I kissed her last night I'd broken down some of these barriers between us. I guess maybe I hadn't done such a good job. "Just answer me, please," I muttered as softly as possible.

"I know what I said to you last night, Leo. And..." She sighed midsentence and then finished her thought. "Yes," she said firmly. "I meant what I said. Every word."

My whole body shuddered. And it wasn't even what she said that had me reeling. Well, yes, her words meant everything. But it was the way she looked at me after she said them. Her eyes were big and wide and waiting. She was looking for my acceptance—for me to reaffirm everything that had happened yesterday. For a moment, I couldn't even respond. We were on the same fucking page…finally…

Then I glanced down at her shirt and immediately lost my train of thought. Her orange t-shirt *did* have scribble on it. It said 'Jesus hates the Yankees' in big black letters. And then, much to my increasing horror, she'd drawn the worst looking Jesus face anyone in existence has ever drawn. "Dammit, what are you wearing?" I demanded. "You have to take that off. Now." Yankee's fans had unequaled pride. And that shirt was just ridiculous and asking for it.

"You want me to strip down naked in front of thousands of people? Pervert," Clara joked.

"I'm serious," I groaned, moving aside to let a family pass us on the steps, trying to use my body as a shield from Clara's horrible shirt as they went past. "You're going to get me slaughtered wearing that. Is that the idea? Is this your latest attempt at murder, killer?"

"Chill out. No one's said a single word to me yet."

"*Yet* being the operative word in that statement. The Orioles are losing. That changes and I'm a dead man."

Clara stopped arguing with me and stared at me intently. I realized I'd just given myself away. Unintentionally, and not in the way I'd wanted to, I'd given her that reassurance her eyes had been longing for a moment ago. I'd told her all over again how much I truly cared. Maybe she and I had a nasty habit of constantly arguing, but I'd beat anyone to a bloody pulp if they ever so much as looked at her funny. She should have already known that—but for the way she looked at me now, this was all new information to her.

Nervous out of my damn mind, I broke eye contact and glanced out at the baseball field. My hand rubbed at the back of my neck and I slowly exhaled—a tactic I used to give myself a moment to think and to calm down. But then I realized something and the new information slammed into me like a bullet to the chest. Clara knew I was a Yankee's fan, or, at the very least, she had to assume I was since I was from New York. So, had she'd worn that shirt to annoy me *on purpose*? Maybe this little arguing thing we did constantly—maybe at some point over the last two days, or even over the past couple years, it had shifted from actual aggression into something completely different. Something a whole lot sexier. Something that completely floored and surprised me.

It also gave me confidence. In general, I was a very confident person. But, like most things, that personality trait kind of went flying out the window when I was with Clara—but with each passing second, more and more, I got the impression that I wasn't flying solo here with my feelings. That knowledge gave me back my self-assurance.

I moved up the final step separating us, narrowing my eyes down at her as she stared back at me. "You wore that shirt to purposely fuck with me," I muttered. "Didn't you?"

"No," she breathed out, seemingly rattled by words and very unconvincing.

"You enjoy fucking with me." It wasn't a question. It was a statement. And my chest turned all gooey inside as I said it. "You have a funny way of flirting with me, Clara. One I never understood until just this moment."

A strand of her hair fluttering across her face as she tried her best to glare at me. But it was a forced glare. "You're delusional and possibly narcissistic," she retorted. "I wore this shirt because I hate the Yankees. It has nothing to do with you."

"Keep telling yourself that, killer," I said softly, moving a little closer to her.

Then gently, because I was scared out of my damn mind here, I brushed that loose strand of her hair out of her face. I tucked it carefully behind her ear. Immediately that pretty little mouth of hers shut up.

"Prove it to me," I whispered, stealing her words from last night. I then cupped her face in my hands and planted one firm kiss on her lips before pulling away. "Prove to me you aren't toying with me," I continued, "that you aren't leading me on like you did with Andrew Wellington, and I'm all yours, baby. All yours."

I hadn't meant for my words to sound sarcastic and I wasn't even fully sure why I'd brought Fuckface Andrew into this. Maybe because it was hard to break old habits with Clara. Or maybe because my insecurities about her relationship with Andrew were trying to break free. So instead of saying anything more, I turned around and moved in the direction of our seats. Then over my shoulder I yelled, “Come sit with me.”

When I reached the very first row, I started shimmying toward the corner of the seating section. *Please follow me. Please follow me.* I repeated those words over and over in my head as I waited to see what Clara would do.

CHAPTER 9:

I plopped down in my empty seat in the front row of our section. Stephany sat two seats over. Clara's empty seat lingered between us.

"You should try *not* arguing with her," she muttered.

"It's hard," I whispered back. "But I am trying."

"Try harder."

A second later, Clara was there. My feet were blocking her way and she was glaring at me. I hadn't even realized I was in her way. I was about to stand to let her pass when suddenly she grabbed the sides of my seat and stepped one leg over my body. She ended up straddling my lap.

What.

The.

Fuck.

My heart expanded to almost painful proportions as her weight settled onto my lap and her hands came to rest on my chest. I don't know what she was playing at or why this was suddenly happening. But she had my full attention. That was for damn certain.

She leaned forward to say something in my ear, quietly so that only I could hear, "Maybe you already know this, since you obviously know everything about me...or maybe I just need to say this for my own good...but I hate Andrew Wellington's effing guts. We went on a few dates, but I have no intention of ever going out with him again. As for the toying—yes, I'm toying with you. But I would never purposely hurt you."

She swallowed hard and then leaned back to look at me. “Understand?”

Words failed me. *Know everything about her?* I hardly knew anything about her. What did that mean? Did she think I knew her well? Did I? I wasn’t sure of anything in this moment. Only the way she felt sitting in my lap, with her legs straddling me—so open, so vulnerable. My hands grew a mind of their own and slipped along her jean covered thighs. Damn. Was this part of her toying or part of the real Clara nobody on this planet had the privilege of truly knowing? I wanted to know that girl. I wanted this to be real, not a game.

Her breathing increased as I studied her. Almost immediately, as if this was too much, as if my close proximity was getting her as aroused as I felt, she sat up to move off me and to go for her seat beside me. But before she could get away, I caught her wrist and motioned for her to come closer. She leaned forward into me.

“That's the sweetest thing you've ever said to me,” I whispered.

The stunned look that coated her face was beyond sexy. I knew immediately that this wasn’t a game. This was real and this was the real Clara. A little vulnerable. A little shy. A little trapped under layers and layers of sarcasm.

I let her go—for now—and she slid into her own seat.

The rest of the game went fine. Conversation was safe, easy, and centered on the game. It felt nice just spending time with her. Clara was witty and easy going. She even got along with Tony and Charlie. But eventually the game had to end. And as we said goodbye to my friends, and Stephany, Clara, and I walked for the nearest stadium exit, I felt this really nice calmness surrounding me.

I felt normal.

“What are your plans for the rest of the day?” I asked her, taking Paul’s advice about prolonging our time. “Are you going back to

Brooklyn?"

"I am," Steph piped up to say. "I have work for my internship that I need to finish tonight."

I eyed Clara intently. "What about you? Are you going with her?"

"I hadn't really thought that far ahead, why?" she asked.

"Because if you aren't going with Steph, then you should spend the rest of the day with me."

There. I said it. I wanted more time with her, simple as that.

"I don't know," Clara muttered.

"Actually," Steph interrupted again, revising her earlier statement. "I have tons of work. Tons and tons. You better take Leo up on his offer. You'll just distract me if you come back with me. And you snore. I got absolutely zero sleep last night."

Smiling, I mouthed a thank you to Stephany as Clara turned to glare in her direction. I'm not sure why, but Clara's friend sure seemed to have my back. That was certainly a first. Most people automatically hated me rather than offering her level of blind support.

"Okay," Clara finally said, giving me the smallest but cutest smile.

So it was agreed. Stephany had to go home to do her homework or something, while I was going to continue this day with the most beautiful girl on the planet. Holy shit. How had I even made this happen? Hell, only two days ago I was on my ass in the grass after she'd ran me over with a golf cart. Now look at me. She'd agreed to a date. Stephany parted ways with us—taking advantage of my town car, letting my driver take her home. And as Clara said goodbye to her friend, I noticed her eyes go wet with unshed tears. It wasn't spoken out loud, and who knows what this meant for me, but it was implied that Clara wouldn't be staying with Stephany for her second night in New York. I assumed that meant she'd be staying at my hotel instead. Obviously, probably in her own hotel room...but a guy could dream.

And as the town car pulled away from the curb, Clara became uncharacteristically quiet. It was just the two of us and she was still battling the tears that wanted to slip out. That pulled at my heart and clenched at my gut. Clara wasn't typically an emotional girl. Actually, I'm not sure if I'd ever seen her cry in recent years. She was hardcore and rock-solid. But, and only for someone very special to her it seemed, she was gooey and soft. It made me fall in love with her just a little bit more.

So I waited, without saying a damn thing for about the first time in my life, for Clara to collect herself. Once she was better, she joked, "So, no one gave me shit about my shirt. Admit it, you were wrong."

I smiled. "Never," I told her softly. "No one gave you shit because your Jesus looks more like Zach Galifianakis. I didn't want to tell you earlier because I didn't want to hurt your artistic feelings, but I bet no one even realized what you were trying to draw."

"Whatever," she laughed, rubbing the last of the evidence away from her eyes. "You realized."

"Well, I'm the exception to the rule," I countered. "And anytime you want to come back to New York to see Steph, I'll take you. Or I can have my jet take you. Whichever."

"Oh," she muttered, surprised by my offer.

Yes, I could be nice when I wanted to be. And yes, I desperately wanted to end this lifelong battle of meanness with Clara and opt for only the nice stuff instead.

"Okay then, let's get out of here." I reached out, grabbing her hand in mine. My fingers intertwined with Clara's and I gently pulled her in the direction I wanted to go. She gave in, letting me take her hand and lead her. "We can't take a cab," I explained, my heart soaring to heights it had never been just holding her hand. I kept talking because my mouth needed to keep moving right this moment. “Trying to catch a cab after a game around here is always a disaster. I could call a car, but that would take forever so I hope you're okay with the subway.”

We reached the subway entrance and headed down the steps. Although the baseball game ended almost thirty minutes ago, there were still people in pinstripes and blue everywhere. I tightened my grip on Clara’s hand, not wanting to risk getting separated. Weaving through the crowd, I led her onto the train’s platform.

“I'm shocked as hell you know how to ride the subway,” Clara suddenly said as we waited for the next train to arrive. “Beyond shocked.”

Rather surprised by her comment, I tried to act casual. Who did she think I was? Richie Rich? Yes, I had the money, but that didn’t mean I’d never set foot on a subway. Despite appearances, I wasn’t a stereotype. “It's just the subway, Clara,” I explained.

“No, it's not just the subway—it’s the whole day. You go to Yankees games, sit in the outfield, have surprisingly regular friends, and then take the subway. Who are you and what did you do with the real Leo Maddox?”

What the hell? Did all this bother her? I inched closer to her body, my eyes narrowing. “Do you find this other side of me *offensive*?”

“No,” she quickly said, her face blanking as she backed down from an argument with me for perhaps the first time ever. “I don’t…the opposite, actually. I like these things about you...a lot. Maybe more than I should.”

Wow. I studied her long and hard for several seconds, both of us breathing just a little too heavy. Wanting to kiss her more than ever, I managed to refrain. I was out of my element with this girl and I didn’t know how to handle that. And when I thought I couldn’t possibly be affected any more, the train pulled into the station and the wind from the movement caused her hair to dance all around her face. Jesus Christ. She was absolutely gorgeous. Like an angel and a demon got together and had the perfect love child. That was Clara. A force to be reckoned with—with the sweetest heart at her center.

Clara's hand dropped from mine as she brushed her wild hair from her eyes. The train doors slid open and quickly she stepped on. I followed. The inside was jammed with people and we had nowhere to sit. Even all the standing room was full. I grabbed a handle bar on the ceiling, waiting to see what Clara would do. At her short height, it was clear she wouldn't be able to reach the handles. Would she use me as a handle instead? I hadn't thought of this dilemma, but instantly I loved it.

The car lurched forward and Clara did not take advantage of me. Instead she bumped into some sweaty, big-bellied, bearded man standing beside her. "Sorry," she muttered and inched away from him. Her eyes met mine and I could tell she was considering grabbing onto me—but somehow she was hesitant.

"It's okay, killer," I told her softly, "I want you to."

Her eyes went wide. "You planned this!"

"What do you mean?" I asked. No, I hadn't planned this, but I should have.

She crossed her arms firmly over her chest. "You planned riding the subway because you knew I would be too short to reach the handles and would have to hold onto you. Newsflash…I happen to have great balance. You just wait and see!"

I kept a straight face. "Okay then."

As the train rounded a corner, she tried to keep steady. But of course, another lurch and she landed right on top of the same man beside her for the second time in a row.

"You trying to feel me up, Missy?" the man asked, winking at her.

"No, sir," she said, rushing to move back in my direction

I threw my head back and laughed. I couldn't help myself. She was too stubborn for her own good. It had been this way our whole lives. And—

All of a sudden, her arms wrapped around my waist and the laugher died in my throat. Because this wasn't just some forced, ass-out hug coming from her. We'd shared plenty of those type of polite pleasantries over the years and this was the opposite of that. She pressed her body into my body, her arms circling me tight, and her fingers digging into the material of my shirt. This was the realest hug she'd given me since we were about six years old.

In an instant I couldn't breathe, move, or speak. My heart was racing away from me. And in this moment, I couldn't help myself—my free hand moved to the back of her head in such a gentle way that it shocked even me. My fingers dug through that long, tantalizing hair of hers and came to rest on her neck. I looked down into eyes that stared wide and big back in my direction. Something about this moment and about our touch took me back in time, to a memory I'd been keeping close to my heart my entire life.

My memory was of a four-leaf clover, a funeral, and a dark library.

And the very moment I fell in love.

For days Maggie had been crying over the loss of her mother, while, the tougher of the two, Clara, reacted differently. She withdrew into herself. I'd always had a similar relationship with both twins—fun, light, and easy. But after Mrs. Ryder passed away, Maggie leaned on me and Clara pushed me away.

On the day of the funeral, as they were lowering the casket into the ground, Clara was off in the grassy field of that graveyard, bent over and searching for something, distant and separated from the rest of the people attending the funeral. My father told me that I ought to talk to her, that the way she was holding her emotions in wasn't normal for a girl, and that I should go keep her company. Reed and Maggie couldn't right that moment and so I needed to go. In my six years of life, if I'd learned one thing, it was to never question my father.

So, I did as I was told.

"What are you doing?" I asked Clara as I approached. Her fingers fluttered over the grass around her. There were no tears on her face. No sign in her eyes that she'd lost her mother only a few days ago. No sadness. No nothing. But all that nothing didn't feel right coming from Clara. She was normally so full of life. I hated seeing her so…emotionless. Even at my age, I understood that just wasn't right for her.

"Nothing," she answered. "Leave me alone."

"My dad told me to come play with you."

She groaned. "Fine. I'm looking for four-leaf clovers. Want to help?"

I shrugged and bent to my knees. If it made her feel better, then I guess I could help her. I thought this was the stupidest, most pointless game she'd ever come up with. And Clara was usually the creative one. But I kept my mouth shut and searched the patch of clovers we were standing in.

"There," I said, spotting one. I pointed but didn't pick it.

Then we proceeded to argue over who should keep it. Frankly, it was a piece of grass and I didn't want it. So in the end, Clara ended up taking it home. I told her to press it in the pages of a book and that would keep it safe. She just stared at me like I was crazy. Then her father called us to come join the others.

That was the saddest day of my life.

But little did I know, things were about to get so much worse. I loved Mrs. Ryder almost as much as my own mother. But two days later, my own mother disappeared in the middle of the night. She packed a single suitcase and took off. No goodbyes or anything. Suddenly, I became just as motherless as Maggie and Clara. It was so strange and so horrible. I couldn't understand what had happened.

"She's gone. She's a selfish bitch and this is for the best anyway. She couldn't handle losing Mrs. Ryder so suddenly and now she needs to go back to the people she thinks 'love' her the most. Whatever. It doesn't matter because you and I are stronger without her."

That was how my father explained the situation to me.

I was shocked. I thought my mom loved me. If she was going to run away, why wouldn't she take me too? It made no sense. It would never make sense to me. But that didn't mean it was any easier for me.

All day I stayed in my room crying. As hard as I tried, I couldn't become emotionless like Clara. I couldn't figure out how she'd detached herself like that. I just couldn't. I wished I knew how to do it, but I felt too much. I wanted to go back in time to when everything was simpler and made sense. Nothing made sense anymore.

My father kept scolding me for crying. Again, bringing up Clara and her ability to hold her emotions in. "If she can do it, then you can. I can't have you moping around like this. It's depressing."

I tried to be strong. I tried and I tried. I was upsetting my father. So when I couldn't stop the sadness, I hid it.

Ten days after Mrs. Ryder died, six days after the funeral, and three days after my mom disappeared—I was sitting in the dark corner of the library, clutching my knees to my chest, silently crying, and hiding from the rest of the world. Suddenly Clara was there in that room with me. The moonlight leaking in through the window revealed her face. I knew it was Clara and not Maggie. I just knew. I always could tell them apart. They looked the same—but then again, they also looked so different.

"I brought you something," she whispered, kneeling down beside me. I was embarrassed that she'd found me like this. I quickly brushed my cheeks with the palms of my hands. But if Clara had noticed my tears, she didn't say anything about them.

She held up that stupid little shamrock by its stem. Had she seriously snuck all the way over to my house, in the middle of the night, because of this plant? "It's the clover we found," she explained as if I couldn't see it for myself. "You can have it now."

"I don't want that," I mumbled. "We decided you were going to keep it safe, remember?"

"I know, but my Mommy's already gone. If you have the clover, then you will be lucky. Then your Mommy will come back."

"My Mom's not coming back," I argued. And she was completely clueless if she believed a clover could bring her back.

Wetness filled her eyes. "Don't say that," she whispered, her voice shaky and broken. She hadn't cried a single tear in the last several days and now she was crying...not for herself, not for her mother...but for me.

That hit my heart like a speeding train.

"Do you wish I would disappear too?" I'm not sure why I asked her this, but I did. I needed to know.

"No," she answered quickly, sounding very shocked and possibly hurt by my words. "Why would I wish that?"

I looked at Clara. I mean really looked at her. And I fell in love with her. It was her kindness I fell in love with. This one small act of kindness.

"I think I do want to keep it," I told her, meaning the clover. "I might need it one day. But we have to hide it because my dad would throw it away if he found it. Have you been keeping it in a book like I told you?"

She nodded.

"Pick a new one in here to hide it in." I pointed to the shelves and shelves of books lining the walls of my dad's library.

Clara sniffled and then stood to her feet. I watched as she wandered around the room, her eyes scanning the books. I watched her in awe, in a new light. She was so different from Maggie—from anyone I'd ever met, actually. I used to think that made her strange, but now I knew otherwise. It made her special.

"Is this one good?" she asked, finally picking a book from the many. I opened the book and tucked the little clover safely between the pages.

"Do you think your dad will read it and find our clover?" she asked.

I put the book back in its place on the shelf. "No. My dad never reads these books."

"Why does he have a giant library if he never reads?"

"The same reason he has eighteen cars."

"Why does he have eighteen cars?"

"You ask too many questions," I muttered to her, not wanting to talk about my dad.

"Can I ask one more?"

"Okay."

"What will you use the clover for?"

That same train-wrecking feeling hit my heart again. "Because," I whispered. "I'm going to ask you to marry me one day, Clara. And I'm going to need all the luck in the world."

"Why?" she demanded. "Don't you want to marry Maggie?"

I couldn't answer her because the library light flipped on and a cold voice reverberated throughout the room, "Leonardo. What are you doing in here?" my father demanded.

"Great Expectations," Clara said aloud, breaking my thoughts and bringing me back to the present.

It took me a second to realize it but we were both thinking of the exact same memory, at exactly the same moment. *Great Expectations*. The book she'd hid the clover in. Many times over the years I'd tried to remember the title to that damn book. I needed to remember so that I could find our clover. I'd searched and searched my father's library—now, since I'd bought the house, *my* library—but I'd never been able to find that book.

"What does that mean?" I asked, but I knew exactly what it meant and, apparently, so did Clara.

"Nothing," she muttered, her face going sheet white. She was remembering how I'd told her I would ask her to marry me one day. I just knew she was. Because I'd never wavered from that wish. And now Clara knew not only that I liked her, but that I always had.

And that scared the hell out of her. The fear on her face was tangible and crippling.

"Don't, Clara," I pleaded. "Stop overthinking this."

"I have to go."

The train stopped at some random destination along our route, the doors slid open, and as people started to move off the train, her arms dropped away from me.

"I'm going back to Steph's. Let me go."

With her eyes lingering on mine, she stepped off that train before I even realized what she was doing. The doors slid closed and suddenly she was gone. One moment we were holding each other and the next moment she was gone. The train moved forward, taking me away from her.

Seriously. What. The. Fuck.

She was gone.

Was this over? Because of one little moment, one little memory…this was over?

CHAPTER 10:

Rip my heart out with a spoon. That would have hurt less. The worst part was I kind of felt like this was coming—like no matter what, in the end, one way or another, I was always going to get my heart ripped out by Clara. She stepped off that train, leaving me high and dry, and it felt like all the progress I'd made with her was lost.

That was almost an hour ago.

My phone buzzed in my pocket. I pulled it out to find a text from Stephany. It said Clara had made it back to her apartment. I was happy she was safe. But I was still feeling absolutely fucking wretched inside.

Not knowing what else to do, since continuing to ride the subway aimlessly didn't seem like an option anymore, I called Paul.

"Hey," I barked as he answered. "It's been a rough day. I feel like shit. I need to get messed up. Where are you at?"

He sighed heavily on the other end. "Charlie said she showed up at the game. He said she was totally into you and seeing you two flirt while he was trying to watch the game was almost nauseating. So, what the hell happened?"

"Nothing a couple of drinks won't fix. Do you want to hit up a bar with me or not?"

"Yeah. I guess so."

I heard it in his voice…worry. Since we'd met on my birthday I'd been a fucking boy scout. I hadn't had more than one drink in a single day. That made me long overdue. My gut was churning and boiling and killing me from the inside out—I needed to do something right the fuck now. Before I truly snapped.

Part of me wanted to call Clara or go to her and say something I know I'd forever regret. I wanted to yell and scream. *Why was loving me so goddamn repulsive?* My mom couldn't be bothered to stick around for me. My dad only tolerated me because I was his prodigy. But Clara...her rejection hurt more than anyone else's.

"Seriously, I urged. "I'm not in good place. I'm going to drink no matter what. So I'd really like some company doing it. I'll pay for your drinks too. Bring your brothers."

"I already agreed, man," Paul told me. "I'll come meet you somewhere. It's no big deal. But is there nothing you can do to fix whatever just happened?"

"Not right this moment. Just meet me."

We agreed on a place, we met thirty minutes later, and I started drinking.

If I was good at one thing in life, it was drinking.

* * *

Four hours later and I forgot why I'd been so upset earlier. Seriously, it was like Clara fucking who?

Well...not really.

But if I kept telling myself that little lie then maybe I would start to believe it. Soon, hopefully. I palmed my bottle of Bud Lite. I typically wasn't into the cheap stuff, but when your goal was to make it so your face went numb and your problems disappeared—you drank whatever went down and sat easiest in your stomach. But as hard as I tried, drink after drink, my mind wouldn't leave Clara. It was mellowing me out. Typically I turned into more a fighter when I drank, not a lover like I was kind of feeling tonight.

"So have you had enough to tell me what happened yet?" Paul urged. Charlie, the only one of Paul's brothers that came along with me today, sat in a booth across the bar. He was talking to a couple of girls, not interested in my moodiness.

"Not drunk enough yet," I told Paul. Unfortunately, I was still fairly level-headed. I had a high tolerance. It would take a few more.

Paul nodded. That worry wasn't as hard on his face anymore. I was managing to keep it together better than I might have expected a few hours ago. Just being around other people kind of helped. Funny how that worked.

"You know," he mused. "I've met Maggie three times now…I think. Yeah, three times. And in all her visits you never mentioned that she had an identical twin. A twin you loved. That's kind of important shit to mention."

I nodded, sighing. "Clara's different though. It's like…I always have this need to protect her. So I don't talk about her much."

At that very moment, my cell phone rang. I fought with my pocket, needing to see who was calling. Shit. As I struggled to get the damn thing out of my pocket, I realized that maybe I was drunker than I thought. I fumbled and squirmed—then dropped my phone on the floor. Finally, speaking of the twins, I got my shit together and saw it was only Maggie calling. Still...I was actually very happy to hear from her.

"Maggie!" I answered with enthusiasm. "What's up, baby doll?"

"Hey, Leo," her familiar voice said. "Where are you?"

"Some bar. Anyway, want to come meet me?"

"I can't. I'm in Blue Creek."

Right. We were states apart. I knew that. “Fuck Blue Creek,” I mumbled.

She giggled. “So what are you doing at *some bar*?”

“I'm out with Paul and his brothers,” I shouted over the noise around me. Paul eyeing me as he sipped his drink. “We're getting drunk and I wish you were here. What are you doing?”

“I'm hiding in a closet, talking to you. Robby is having dinner with us. He has a daughter. They're both out on the back deck right now and I'm in the closet.”

That Rat Bastard! What the hell! A daughter? And the asshole still had time to try to hit on Maggie? And there went the lover in me. Just hearing Robby’s named turned me back into the fighter. I tried to jump to my feet but proceeded to fall straight on my ass. Not good. I was cutting myself off after this. Paul laughed and helped me to my feet.

“Mags!” I shouted into my phone. “I told you to wait for me. I told you I would take care of him. What the hell is he doing at your house?”

“Good question. It's been a crazy day.”

“I'll say. Well, get out of the closet and tell that fucker to go home. Don't say ‘fucker.’ Not with his daughter there and all, but go tell him to get his ass off your back deck—I mean it. He has no right to be there. He lost that right a long time ago.”

“Where's Clara?” she asked. “Are you with her?” Her change of subject was obviously meant to distract me away from Robby…and it worked.

“Brooklyn,” I muttered.

“That's a vague answer, Leo. Elaborate, please.”

I covered the phone with my hand, rolling my eyes at Paul. “I’ve got go talk to Maggie outside for a moment. I need air.”

He simply nodded.

I walked across the bar, stepping through the door and outside onto the busy sidewalk. The sun was sinking and everything had an orange tint to it. People passed me in a rush, going about their random lives, and I ignored it all and talked to my friend.

"I don't know what the hell I'm doing," I answered Maggie honestly. "You should have seen the way Clara ran away from me on the subway today...like I butchered her dog. Dammit. There's such a fine line between love and hate. Do you think it's possible to fall for someone after you've spent a lifetime hating them?"

It took Maggie a moment but then she responded. "I'm not sure if it's because you're drunk or what, but what kind of question is that? If you love someone, you just love them. Flaws and all. You can't hate someone and love them at the same time—it doesn't work that way. Love is all or nothing. Sometimes your own issues get in the way, but once you strip away all the noise, you find that there is just love underneath."

Wow.

"Who knew you were so insightful?" I told her, half-joking but mostly serious. "So what you're saying is...if Clara likes me, then it's not possible for her to genuinely hate me at the same time? It's an either/or kind of thing?"

My whole life I'd assumed Clara hated me. I'd spent a lifetime saying lots of stupid shit I didn't mean to the girl. Why wouldn't she hate me? I was mean because I was scared. I was scared of myself and those feelings that had hit my fragile six-year-old heart that night in that library. I pushed her away because I never wanted her to hurt me the way my mother had hurt me. I pushed and pushed, but the simple truth was—Clara was and would always be *it* for me. And if there was even a smidgeon of a chance that hate wasn't the only thing in her heart, then I needed to see her.

Now.

"I have to go," I shouted into the phone. "There's somewhere I need to be. Now go tell Robby to get off your deck. Please. I'll see you tomorrow and we can deal with him together. Okay?"

"Okay. Always, Leo."

"Always," I answered. Then I hung up and whistled as loud and as hard as I could for an approaching taxi.

CHAPTER 11:

This was it. Do or die.

When I fell off that balcony two and a half years ago, deciding after that night that I needed to get my life in order, it was all in preparation for this moment. And when I jumped in front of Clara's moving golf cart that too was for this moment.

Showered, freshly clothed, with a couple hours of time to let the alcohol begin to leave my system, I sat in the backseat of my car, my driver eyeing me suspiciously from the front seat, outside Stephany's apartment in Brooklyn. It was late. Very late. It had taken me way too long, metaphorically and physically speaking, to get myself over here. I was debating on whether I should speak with Clara now or wait until the morning.

Fuck it, I decided, jumping out of my car. Enough bullshitting around. I needed to see her *now*. It couldn't wait any longer. I didn't care if I woke her up and the whole damn neighborhood. The only thing on my mind was speaking with her. If she was feeling any of the things I was feeling then she shouldn't have run away from me earlier. I know Clara has a thing about bolting when the shit hit the fan, but I wanted to be her one exception. I wanted her to run to me, not away from me, when things got hard.

Hurrying across the street and up the steps to Stephany's place, my heart pounded against my ribs so hard that I could barely see straight. Did Clara even feel a fraction of what I was feeling? Not knowing was the hardest part. At the stadium earlier, for the smallest moment—it had felt real. When we kissed the night before—it had felt real. And on the subway, when we both remembered the same memory of the clover—it had felt real. And as I paused, my hand ready to knock on Stephany's door, my whole being ready to put it all on the line—it felt real.

And then suddenly, like the answer to all my frantic stressing, my phone began to buzz in my pocket. Who could be calling at this hour? It was past two in the morning. Only one person could possibly be calling. I was too damn afraid to even take my phone out of my pocket to check to make sure it was her. The buzzing stopped and then immediately started again. And then…the door to Stephany's place swung wide open.

There she was.

Holy hell, Clara. She was insanely gorgeous.

The first thing I noticed were her tits. Sweet Jesus. All she wore was a tank-top without a bra and I was a guy so it was impossible for my eyes *not* to go straight to her chest. And even though it was a hot evening, her nipples were tight and straining against the thin fabric. Shit. My eyes wandered further over her perfect little body and…double shit. She didn't have pants on either, only a pair of black panties. Was this how she normally dressed for bed? I hoped so. Was this how she normally answered doors in the middle of the night in Brooklyn? I hoped not.

I was about to scold her for being so naive and stupid. We weren't in Blue Creek. She couldn't just answer the door so scantily clad! What if I were some axe-murder rapist whom had just shown up on her door step?

But as my mouth opened to tell her exactly what I thought of her body teasing the whole neighborhood, my eyes came to meet hers. Immediately I shut my damn mouth. Because there wasn't a single ounce of anger staring back at me. There was something else there. Lust. Pure, hot, rip-my-clothes-off-and-fuck-me-twenty-ways-to-Sunday lust. And it was all being directed at me.

Neither of us said a word, but the tension between us was thick with feelings, emotions, and a whole lot of want. Letting out a long, slow exhale, I rubbed one hand over the back of my neck. I did this as a way to distract myself from the beautiful girl standing in front of me. My entire body wanted nothing more than to grab her face and kiss her into morning, but I was trying my damnedest to be the gentleman I really wasn't.

And then it happened, Clara flinched in my direction. And there went my control. Without another second of hesitation, my hands caught her neck and drew her in close to me. We came together in a kiss to end all kisses. It was wild. It was desperate. It was everything to me.

To hell with everything else. I pressed my body flush with hers, backed her against the door frame, and pinned her in place with my hips. She gasped when she felt my erection pressing into her.

Yes, I was fucking turned on.

Yes, I was hard enough to do damage.

Yes, I needed her to know exactly the effect she had over my body.

"Don't ever run away from me like that again," I whispered as I kissed a trail down her neck. "You can talk to me. You can *always* talk to me, okay? It's not like I'm going to bite." And then, much to my own surprise, I dragged my teeth along her sweet skin and gently nipped her.

She squealed and gave my chest a playful smack. "You ass!"

"Whatever. You like it."

I still had her pinned in place, my hips square with hers. What surprised me most was how tenderly Clara returned all my touches. And then at one point, she even rubbed her hands up and over my shoulders, pausing at my neck. She studied me for a long moment, and then the next thing I knew, her hands were yanking me in for another kiss.

I abruptly pulled back, remembering that my driver could see me from where he was parked. “Inside?” I asked.

She nodded, so I slid my hands down and grabbed her scantily covered ass. I lifted Clara up and into my arms effortlessly. Her legs were strong as she wrapped them around my waist. Carrying her through the doorway, I found the inside of Stephany's apartment to be pitch black. I walked into the unknown as Clara peppered my face and neck with little, light kisses.

My heart expanded and nearly exploded. Making-out was one thing. But these little kisses were something else entirely. They were gentle and soft. It occurred to me then that she was loving on me, caring on me—something I’m not sure I’d ever experienced before.

“Shit,” I yelped as my leg banged into something. It was too dark to see and I’d been walking blindly, too focused on the girl in my arms and her sweet way of kissing me.

Clara laughed softly. “Couch,” she whispered against my ear.

As if by magic, I bumped into the couch next. Thank God. I lowered Clara down onto cushions I could barely see and then covered her body with my own. I adored the feel of Clara underneath mine. Her chest pressed into my chest. Her heartbeat raced in tune with my own. Her legs locked tightly back around my waist. And she shifted around until her sweet spot lined up with my own.

Oh, God.

In a heartbeat, I shifted all my weight off her and jumped back to sit on the other end of the couch as if I’d just touched fire. I couldn’t do this. My inhibitions were a little off because I still had a fair amount of alcohol in my system. It was too damn dark and Clara was too damn irresistible. No matter what, I couldn’t fuck her tonight. Not tonight. Not like this.

No.

Matter.

What.

“What are you doing?” she asked, pushing up on her elbows to glare from the other side of the couch. Her words had a warning laced through them. “Get back over here, please,” she demanded.

“I can't.”

“Then what do you even want?” she groaned, but I didn’t miss the small amount of hurt in her voice. “You're confusing the hell out of me, Leo.”

“I just want you,” I whispered. I didn’t want her to think I was rejecting her by not continuing whatever was about to happen between us. The opposite, actually. “I want you more than my next breath. Believe me, Clara. It would be very easy to lay you back down, ease myself inside you, and fuck you senseless. But I can't just screw you on some random couch where anyone could walk in on us. And I can't screw you while the room is spinning and I'm slightly shitfaced. I don't even want to screw you. I want to make love to you. The slow, sweet, all night long kind of love.” I sighed and buried my face in my hands for a moment. “I can't believe I just said that out loud, but...” I paused and stared back at her, “it's true.”

She stared at me blankly. I wondered which of my words had shocked her the most.

“Say something, Clara,” I urged. The silence was killing me.

“Get back over here, please,” she repeated.

I groaned. “I just told you why I can't.”

“Yeah, I know. I'm not asking you to screw me. I've spent a lifetime *not* touching or holding you...and I really want to now. Besides, it's kind of cold over here without you.”

Oh. Well, okay then.

I moved back to where I belonged. Our legs tangled together as we adjusted and got comfy. I ended up on my side with her nuzzled in close to my body. She rested her head in the nook of my arm. It was getting even later and we were both tired.

I realized then that we were…cuddling. Like, you know, that thing that real, live couples do. I couldn't believe it. Clara was kissing me and being gentle with me. 'Loving on me,' if you will. This was real. This was everything I'd ever wanted from her. I didn't need to have sex with her to be close to her. I only needed to hold her.

But that didn't mean I still wasn't toying with temptation. As we held onto each other and remained close, I refrained from kissing her for the time being. I ran my mouth along her jaw and tenderly traced my fingers over her stomach, just under her shirt, but I didn't kiss her sweet, tempting lips anymore.

"Can I stay the night?" I whispered.

"I assumed you were going to," she answered.

"Good."

I sat up briefly, yanking off my shirt. She'd mentioned she was cold and that simply wouldn't do. I used my shirt to cover as much of her legs as I possibly could. "Are you still cold?" I asked as I lay back down beside her.

She laughed into my chest, inhaling against me. "I'll manage, thanks."

My arms squeezed her tighter. And then, much to my increasing surprise, Clara inhaled against me again. What?

"I might be a little drunk and imagining things, but are you *sniffing* me?" I asked her, needing to know for certain.

"Nope."

"It kind of feels like you are."

"Nope." And then playfully she inhaled against my chest for the third time.

That's it. I'd entered the fucking twilight zone. Clara was sniffing me and cuddling with me. Yeah, I was pretty sure any moment I would wake up from this wonderful dream and find myself all alone in a sterile, cold hospital bed with head trauma.

"You know what's weird?" Clara said a few minutes later as we were both starting to drift off to sleep. I'd been trying my hardest to stay awake, but the late hour had finally caught up with me. "I can never tell when you're drunk and when you aren't."

Wow. That hit me hard and woke me back up. I faked being drunk all the damn time and no one—I mean, *no one*—had ever noticed. Or…*bothered* to notice.

"That's because I'm usually faking it," I whispered honestly.

One of her fingers was lazily tracing along the bare-naked skin of my chest. It felt nice. Way too nice. "What's that supposed to mean?" she asked.

"It means that every time you see me with one of those Gibson Martinis—the kind with the onion that I'm always drinking—it's really just water. Doug at the club is cool. He hooks me up."

Clara pressed her palms against my chest. "Wait a minute. Does that mean you were sober when I hit you with the golf cart?"

I almost laughed, but I couldn't tell if she was angry with me or not. "Yes," I answered.

"I carried your heavy ass up to your room and you were perfectly fine?"

"Yes."

And then the girl bit me. She flat out bit me. I can't believe she had the guts to do such a thing. Sure I'd nipped her before when we were making out in the doorway, but she full on bit me. I think hard enough to leave a mark too. Oh, now this was war. I flipped her onto her back, easily pinning both her small hands above her head with my larger one, and used my free hand to tickle the shit out of her. She squealed in fun, obviously not really mad about my 'fake drunk' thing.

I didn't even care if I woke up Stephany and whoever else might live in this little apartment, I continued tickling Clara until she cried for me to stop. Our tickling war ended with me on top and straddling her waist, still pinning her hands above her head. I was so much stronger than her, she never stood a chance against me. I stared down at her small body under me, my chest repeatedly rising and falling hard.

This was totally something Clara and I would do.

"Say you're sorry, killer," I muttered as I bent over to press wet kisses all over her face.

She squirmed under me. "Never."

"Fine." Instead of continuing our game, I instead pressed my lips lightly against hers. Getting to kiss her was my new favorite thing. Our tongues met and came together in a way that sent a shiver straight to my already hard cock. Shit. I pulled off of her, shifting us around so that I lay beside her rather than on top.

"We should go to sleep before I break all the boundaries I'm trying to keep with you," I explained, planting one more kiss on her forehead.

"One more thing," she whispered. "Tell me why you fake the drinking thing. Please."

I sighed, but proceeded to tell her without filter. "I used to get shitfaced like it was my job. In high school mostly. Then I stopped because drinking would always take me down a very dark rabbit hole. I did a lot of stuff I'm not proud of. Stuff that would make your skin crawl. Stuff that's hard to live with now. I hated myself and I guess I needed an alternative..." I paused for a moment, thinking over exactly how to explain this.

"People still expect me to act a certain way, and I keep up the act because it's easier to pretend. Or maybe I just like messing with people. I don't know."

"Does Maggie know this?" she asked.

"She doesn't."

"I won't tell. But Leo...why did you just tell me? You didn't have to."

"You asked." One of my hands moved to cup her face. "I don't know why, but I always have to be honest with you. You bring it out in me somehow. It's a very scary but liberating feeling. There's no pressure to be anyone but myself when I'm with you. And getting to spend so much time with you over the last couple days...well, I've never felt so free in my life. I'll tell you anything you want to know, Clara. Just tell me we won't ever go back to where we were three days ago."

"We won't," she confirmed, emotion thick in her voice.

"Good," I answered quickly before I had the chance to get emotional here too. "We can talk more tomorrow. Let's go to sleep now, killer."

So we did.

CHAPTER 12:

Whispers woke me. I'd fallen asleep with Clara in my arms and happiness exploded in my heart when I found her still in my arms.

"I told you," someone whispered, probably Stephany. "I told you he wouldn't be able to stay away from you long. I knew he was crazy about you. Now you owe me twenty bucks."

Keeping my eyes pinned shut, not wanting either girl to know I was awake and listening just yet, I stayed perfectly still, waiting to see if Clara would say anything in response to her friend's comments. She said nothing. Instead I felt her nestle a little closer into my chest.

"Anyway," Stephany whispered. "I need to finish getting ready. You should get up soon unless you want my roommates drooling all over Leo. And who knew he was so religious? It's hot."

I heard the sound of heels walking away on the hardwood floor, so I knew Stephany had left us. She'd called me religious because of my tattoos. Most of the ones covering my chest, back, and shoulders had some sort of religious undertone to them. The ironic part was, I wasn't really all that religious. I just liked what I liked.

"I'm not *that* religious," I muttered, my voice rough with sleep. My eyes were still closed tight and part of me was afraid to open them. What if Clara didn't look at me the same way she had last night? What if in the few hours we'd been asleep, she'd come to her senses and realized she wanted nothing to do with me?

Finally, I stopped being a pussy about this whole situation, and just opened my damn eyes. My worries were instantly put at ease. Clara's bare legs were tangled with mine, her hands were curled up under her face, and her gray eyes were big and staring straight into mine. At our eye contact, her cheeks flushed pink. I felt that flush all over my entire body.

Now *that* was an image I wanted to wake up to every morning. I was about to tell her how beautiful she was in the morning but she spoke first.

"Um, you look good," she mumbled. And then, as if her words had embarrassed her, the girl who never let anything affect her, immediately buried her face into the cushions of the couch.

She was so damn adorable.

I cupped her face in my hands and forced her to look at me. The biggest smile came to my lips. I couldn't really help myself. "Don't get shy on me," I whispered and rocked my hips into her hips, showing her how very *not* shy I was at that moment.

Not giving a rat's ass about anything or anyone but us, I pressed my lips to hers and stole a kiss. And then another. Then another. My fingers moved to her waist, tracing along the edge of her panties, tempting and teasing us both. I really wanted to touch her more and I was having the hardest time not giving in to all my urges.

"Why is there a naked man on my couch?" came a voice from across the room.

At hyper-speed, Clara pulled away from my grip and scrambled off the couch. I sighed at the cold rush of air I felt in her absence. Another girl, who I assumed was a roommate to Stephany, had her eyes narrowed at Clara. She needed to calm down. It's not like we'd been screwing on her couch. And besides, I was far from naked. I still had on my shoes.

"This is Leo," Clara told the other girl. "I hope it's okay that he stayed over. We're gonna leave as soon as Steph is ready for work."

Her lips pursed for a short moment. "Whatever." She shrugged and went for the coffeemaker in the kitchen, mumbling, "You could at least put some pants on and stop showing off your boyfriend."

Clara turned toward me, pretending like she hadn't heard the other girl refer to me as her boyfriend. But whatever, either way, I liked the sound of that. It was far too soon to cross that bridge but maybe one day. I smiled. Yes, one day. It all seemed within reach now. I stood up, grabbed my shirt off the couch, and yanked it over my head in one quick motion.

Clara blatantly stared at me as I did this. She was checking me out. And if I wasn't mistaken, she liked what was in front of her. Walking to her, I planted a kiss on her forehead. I said nothing as she stared up at me.

"I'm sorry I never noticed you before," she suddenly blurted out, her voice shaky. "I'm sorry I was mean to you over the years. Because I was. You were meaner, but...I could have been nicer. And I'm sorry I ran away from you on the subway. That was just rude. And in high school—even when we only saw each other over holidays and summers—I knew you were in a dark place. I knew something was wrong with you and that all your fucked-up-ness was really just some giant plea for help." Tears formed in her eyes. "I'm sorry because I knew and I looked the other way and—"

I stopped her words with a kiss.

She kept trying to talk. "Leo—"

"Stop it." I circled my arms around her shoulders and squeezed her tight against my chest. She was so petite and felt so good pulled in close against me. I leaned into her, burying my face between her neck and shoulder, taking a very deep breath. She smelled like strawberries and summer… and home. "None of it matters. I'm better and you're here now.

None of it matters," I assured her.

I didn't even know all that was true until I just now said it out loud. I *was* better. I wasn't the same reckless kid I'd once been. I had the girl I'd always wanted in my arms and it made me feel invincible. Like that recklessness inside of me suddenly had purpose.

"Where are your pants?" I whispered after a few moments. "As much as I like you without them, I need you dressed so we can get out of here. Where's Stephany?"

"I'm here," Steph said from behind us. "Sorry I keep barging in on your moments, but I really need to leave for work now or I'm going to be late."

Clara broke out of my grip, nodding briefly in Stephany's direction before hurrying from the living room.

"She's a hot mess, that one," Stephany muttered while Clara was gone. "I mean that in the best possible way. One hot mess and it's all your fault. It might not seem like it on the surface, but that giant heart of hers…it's all yours. Don't mess it up now."

My own heart thumped as I listened to Stephany and waited for Clara. I didn't know how to respond to that. But I didn't have to. A second later Clara rushed back into the living room—yesterday's clothes on and ready to go. The three of us left the apartment and began walking down the street.

"I guess this is goodbye again," Stephany told Clara as we neared my black town car. I noticed my driver sleeping in the front seat. I'd have to give him a big tip and possibly a raise after putting him through last night's ordeal.

Stephany hugged Clara tight, muttering something in her ear. Then she surprised the hell out of me when she let go of Clara only to catch me in an equally big hug. She was tall and nearly my same height. Awkwardly, but forever thankful for her help this weekend, I returned her hug. Then she let go and set off down the street.

I think I had a new friend too. Imagine that.

I took a deep breath, took Clara's hand in mine, and, without a single word, led her over to my town car, held the door for her, and followed her into the vehicle.

"JFK," I told my driver. Then, still exhausted from barely sleeping last night, slumped way down into my seat, getting comfy. I motioned for Clara to come to me. And she did. She snuggled in close to my chest. She turned my right arm over and gently traced her fingers over my little scar. That loving quality about her—it was my absolute favorite thing on this earth. I'd seen it once when we were kids. But seeing it now... was something amazing.

"I'm flying home commercially," she informed me.

This was news to me. That meant she'd had to have bought her own ticket. I tensed involuntarily, suddenly uneasy and questioning her loving touch. Her words and her touch didn't match.

"I booked the ticket yesterday when I wasn't so sure about us," Clara continued on. "You came over and everything's different, but I still want to go home on my own. Maggie already agreed to pick me up from Roanoke, and I need the two-hour car ride with my sister to try to smooth things over with her. Or at least attempt to. For this thing—whatever is happening between us—to even have a shot at working out, then I need to be on better terms with your best friend. You get what I'm saying?"

My body automatically relaxed. I'd been mistaken. Her words and her touch matched perfectly. "You'd try to make peace with your sister for me?"

"Yes."

"Okay then." Wow. Seriously, wow. A life time battle between sisters and Clara was ready to call it quits all for me? Wow. Still—I wished she wasn’t flying commercially. “Can I at least walk you to your gate when we get to JFK?” I asked.

“Okay then,” she repeated, shifting in my arms to get a better look at me. “Um, how exactly are you going to get through security without a ticket?”

A grin spread over my lips. “I'm Leo Maddox. I'm pretty sure I can handle it.”

She laughed. “Whatever, you ass.”

I smiled wider. I liked how she always called me on my bullshit.

We reached the airport and my driver dropped us off at the curb. I popped open the trunk and pulled out Clara’s bag of stuff. We entered the airport. And while she printed her ticket from a kiosk, I bought a ticket to Boston on my phone. It didn’t matter where my ticket said I was going because I only needed to get through security to walk her to her gate. And, yes, I would spend five hundred dollars on a last minute ticket to do just that. After I finished, I glanced up to find Clara not-so-subtly staring at me. It made me smile. I was doing a lot of that today. I grabbed her hand, lacing our fingers together, and we walked in silence toward security.

After we made it through security and to her gate, we found they had already begun boarding the flight. This was why I hated commercial flights. They never took off when they were supposed to, except on the days you wished they wouldn’t.

“Did you just buy a ticket so you could walk me to my gate?” she asked, squeezing my hand and narrowing her eyes up at me. “You shouldn't have done that. I would have been perfectly fine alone.”

“I know, but I wanted to walk you,” I admitted.

“You're ridiculous. Kind of sweet, but still ridiculous.”

“I'd buy a thousand tickets for the chance to spend a few extra minutes with you. To be honest, I'm a little worried that at any moment I'm going to wake up and this will have all been a dream—you'll hate me again, and I'll still be stuck trying to figure out how to change that. So, yeah, of course I'm going to try to prolong the moment."

At my words, Clara grabbed my neck and pulled my lips to hers. My mouth was partially open and she caught me off guard. I sucked in a sharp breath and instantly gave into her kiss, which was passionate, tender, and mixed with lots of emotions. This kiss was so much more than a goodbye kiss.

Final boarding call for US Air Flight 833 to Roanoke. Final boarding call.

Dammit, they were calling her flight. Clara quickly pulled out of my grip, before I even had a moment to protest, and she left me to board the plane. But then at the last second, she turned back around and rushed back in my direction.

And in a move that was beyond dramatic, but something that embodied Clara's personality and that I loved, she leapt up into my arms. Her legs locked around my waist and again she kissed me. She kissed me and held onto me like we weren't in a crowded airport, like we were the only two people present. Hell, the only two people left on this earth.

"Fuck, Clara," I growled into her sweet mouth. My hands tangled into her long hair, and I had no choice but to meet her kiss with equal intensity. "You're making me want to strip you naked and have my way with you right here on the airport floor." I set her down, her feet hitting solid ground. "Now get your sexy ass on that plane. Please."

She rolled her eyes. Actually rolled her eyes at me. "Just so you know...if you're dreaming, then I'm dreaming too. And I'm going to make sure you never wake up," she promised. Then she left me and boarded the plane.

I stood and stared at the spot she'd disappeared from for about thirty seconds. Then I raced through that airport. I had to get back to Blue Creek.

Now.

* * *

The closest major airport to Blue Creek was the Roanoke Airport. And Roanoke was a good two hour drive from Blue Creek. I arrived in my dad's jet at the Blue Creek local airstrip with only about a ten minute drive ahead of me. So I knew I had about a two hour head start on Clara. I needed that time to speak with Reed.

Because I was going to ask for his permission to date his daughter.

I went straight to his house. After knocking and knocking on the front door, I came to the conclusion that Maggie had already left to pick Clara up and Reed wasn't home. But I had a key of my own, so I let myself inside.

Yep, no one was home. It was very eerie being in the Ryder house all alone. And I was about to leave when I spotted a note on the counter. It read:

Clara,

We're having a family dinner tonight. Six sharp. Also, I scheduled you to work today at 11:00. Check in with Mary Ann at the Pro Shop. You'll be giving golf lessons. Dress appropriately please and don't make a scene with Mary Ann.

Love,

Your (very angry but trying to keep his cool) Dad

I had no idea why Reed would be 'angry and trying to keep his cool' with Clara. She'd been in New York with me. Maggie came to visit me all the time. What the fuck was his problem having Clara come with me? I wasn't sure, but it left a sour feeling in the pit of my stomach. If I told him that I wanted to date her, would he even allow it? He better because I wasn't going to take no for an answer.

Leaving the Ryder's house, I marched across the golf course. If I knew Reed (and I did) then I knew he'd already be golfing. I went straight for the Pro Shop because he'd mentioned it in that letter to Clara. My trek across the mile of grassy course ruined yet another pair of my favorite shoes.

Mary Ann was a bitch. I'd never cared for her. But I usually hated most people, so maybe she wasn't as bad as she seemed. Who the hells knows. I came into the Pro Shop to find her and a small crowd gathered around a speaking Reed. He noticed me enter the room, pausing his speech for a moment to nod in my direction, before continuing on with whatever he was saying.

"So anyway, Clara will be giving away free golf lessons this week and next. If anyone wants to sign up for a one hour time slot, here is the signup sheet." He set a clipboard down on Mary Ann's desk. "The times start at eleven this morning. If you could pass the word along for her, I'd appreciate it."

What the fuck? I was damn near positive that Clara wasn't going to want any part of this. Golfing was something Maggie, Clara, and I had all been raised on. But Clara, the most talented of the three of us, didn't golf anymore. In fact, at her high school graduation party, she'd had a huge blow up at her dad, where she basically told him to his face she'd never golf again. And she hadn't. To my knowledge she hadn't picked up a golf club since that day. The worst part of it was, she used to love golf—so much that I knew her refusal to play was merely a giant *fuck you* to her father. But still, either way, I felt like Reed had no right springing this on her.

Pressing my way through the small crowd, I took the clipboard first. "Hi, Reed," I muttered, signing my name at the very top of his list. When Clara showed up for her first lesson today—*if* she showed up for her first lesson—it would be me she'd find. And she wouldn't have to golf with me if she didn't want to. Hell, golfing was about the last thing I wanted to do with Clara.

Then I passed the clipboard to Mr. Sinclair, an elderly man who'd been a member at the club for years, and turned my attention back to Reed.

"Hi, Leo," he said to me. "Are you okay? I heard Clara ran you over with a golf cart after Friday's party. I'm sorry she's been acting out lately and took her anger out on you. I'm going to have a serious talk with her when she gets home from New York this morning. She can't keep pulling this shit. And don't even get me started on her ordeal with Andrew Wellington. That boy has been by the house five times this weekend looking for her. He's beginning to rub me the wrong way."

The man was clueless—*fucking* clueless. And I laughed out loud because of it. "Clara was with me in New York this weekend, Reed. And whatever was going on with her and Andrew…well, it's definitely finished now."

It better be over with her and Andrew. And I assumed it was given the way last night went.

"Oh," Reed muttered, running one of his tanned hands through his thick blond hair, and staring at me. He understood exactly what I was saying.

"Yeah. Oh," I repeated. Nervousness prickled through me as I waited for his response. Hardly ever did I care what someone thought of me—but I cared what Reed thought.

Then he smiled. I mean really, genuinely smiled. And he squeezed my shoulder for a brief second before walking toward the exit.

"Wait," I called after him. "Aren't you going to say anything else?"

"No." He shrugged, turning back in my direction. "Is there something I should say?"

"Aren't you going to say you always expected Maggie and me to end up together? Isn't that what everyone always says?"

"Leo…I've never expected you to end up with Maggie." And then he walked out that door, his golf shoes clicking on the wood floor of the Pro Shop, leaving me completely dumbfounded. That went surprisingly well. *And I didn't even have a chance to ask him anything!*

With about an hour to kill before I expected Maggie and Clara to return from the airport, I headed over to the valet parking. I'd left my car there several days ago and it was about time I picked it up.

CHAPTER 13:

Dammit. *Who the hell owns so many random books?*

I swear to God, I'd already found three different copies of Great Expectations in my father's library. Correction, *my* library. And none of them were *the* copy. None of the books I'd found had that little clover tucked inside the pages. I think I was losing my damn mind looking for this thing. Clara had mentioned the name of that book and now I desperately needed to find it.

When I'd bought this house from my father, I'd bought it with every intention of tearing the place apart, remodeling, and turning it into my own place. So far, I'd done none of that. And…well, now I suddenly had a million impulses to do what I'd always wanted to do. And I guess starting in the library was as good of a place as any.

Of all the rooms in this house, the library was one of the spots I wanted to keep the same. Mostly because of that one memory I shared with Clara inside this room. But most of the books filling this library needed to go. They were random. Most of them duplicate copies. Probably bought only to fill the shelves. So as I searched for this clover, I started sorting out the books I wanted to get rid of. An hour easily slipped by as I fell into an easy rhythm, searching and sorting. And as it neared eleven o'clock and my appointment with Clara, I hurried upstairs to change into the proper golf attire.

I'd just finished getting dressed, in a white golf shirt and khaki pants, when the buzzer on the front gate sounded through the house—alerting me to the fact that someone was here.

And, low and behold, it was Robby who appeared on the video screen showing off the front gate.

Did he even have a brain in that thick skull of his? Couldn't he leave Maggie the hell alone already? He really wanted to start shit, didn't he? I buzzed him through the gate and headed outside to meet the asshole. My temper and my heart rate were both flaring as I charged down the stone steps, toward my driveway. What was he trying to prove?

His truck pulled close to where I stood.

"Look Leo," he said, opening the door to his truck and hopping out. His brown hair was floppy and messy and today he wore his facial hair scruffy. He'd been more clean-cut the night of the gala, but today he looked more like the Robby I used to remember. Well, the taller version of that Robby. "I know that you don't want to hear this," he started to say. "But—"

My cell phone was ringing, interrupting whatever pathetic speech he was about to give me. I'd turned it off vibrate in case Clara tried calling me today. And as I went to answer it, I noticed that it was nearly eleven. Fuck Robby. I didn't have time for his bullshit right now.

Ironically though, it was Maggie who was calling. So I answered immediately.

"Hey, Mags. You won't believe who—" I started to say to her, glaring at Robby as I spoke.

"Did you know about Andrew?" she blurted out, cutting me off, her voice a little frantic. "Did you know about him cheating on me?"

"What?" I asked. Maggie sounded as if she was on the verge of crying.

I motherfucking hated Andrew Wellington, but I never knew he'd cheated on Maggie while they were together. I turned away from Robby to ask, "Cheating when?"

"I don't know. Something like the entire last year we were together."

"I'm at my house. Come over. Now, Mags."

"Okay. I'll be right there," she whispered and then her line went dead.

I figured, being that Maggie had driven Clara home from the airport, that Clara must have been the one to inform Maggie of Andrew's infidelity. I guess I wasn't too surprised to find out that Fuckhead was a cheater on top of being an asshole. But why would Clara, knowing this about Andrew, ever go for him? It made no sense.

"Was that Maggie on the phone?" Robby asked. I'd nearly forgotten about him standing there with me.

"Yes," I muttered, still in shock. "And she's on her way over. Right now. And she's upset."

"Is she upset because of me?"

"No, you dipshit. Not because of you. She has other issues in life and none of them revolve around you. So you should stop trying to convince yourself that any of us even remotely care about you or where you've been for the last six years."

The next moment Maggie's red car pulled into my driveway. It screeched to a dramatic halt a few feet away from me. She stepped out of the car and I moved across the pavement to catch her in a hug. Maggie was like a little sister to me. I always looked out for her. I always protected her. Because she'd always needed me to. And it hurt me whenever I failed at that job. Sometimes I wished she had Clara's tough exterior, but she didn't.

"I didn't know about Andrew," I whispered to her. "I'm so sorry. Who told you this?"

"Clara," she whispered back, confirming what I already knew.

"Why would Clara date Andrew if she knew that?" I growled, pulling away from Maggie. Suddenly *I* felt just as hurt as Maggie looked. Was everything that had happened between Clara and me some sort of lie too? Some sort of game. I couldn't make sense of why she'd decided to date Andrew on a whim. Was she doing the exact same dramatic bullshit with me too?

"Fuck this. Fuck me," I mumbled to myself. "I still can't make sense of her and Andrew together." I ran my hands through my hair, pulling at the ends. "One moment it feels like she's all in with me and then in the next moment…everything comes back to fucking Andrew all over again."

Maggie sighed. "Leo, calm down. Clara hates Andrew too," she explained. "Just like you thought. She thinks he's a *lying pig who kisses like a Dachshund*. Or was it a Doberman? She also said something about wanting to protect me while giving Andrew a taste of his own medicine, but she couldn't date him while she had feelings for you. She wasn't mean to me today on the car ride home from the airport. She may have told me a bunch of stuff I didn't want to hear, but overall she was a lot nicer than she's been in years. I'm pretty sure you have everything to do with that. So stop pacing like a trapped animal—it's making me dizzy. And don't pull at your hair like that or you're going to go prematurely bald."

I stopped moving from where I'd unknowingly been walking in circles. My hands moved from my hair and fell to my sides. So Clara wasn't playing me? The relief I felt almost knocked me over. I let out a giant breath and then started moving up the steps to my house.

"Where are you going?" Maggie called after me.

"The library. I was working on a project before *Dan* here interrupted me. So get rid of loverboy and then come find me," I told her and disappeared into the house.

The thing with Robby, aka Dean, was this—I wasn't entirely sure

Maggie didn't want him back in her life. Sure, I still thought he was shady as hell and up to no good. But if Maggie wanted him gone, she was going to either have to tell me to get rid of him or do it herself. It occurred to me then that she'd done neither as of yet.

Making my way through the house and into the library, I picked up a book and started flipping. It wasn't the one I needed, so I threw it onto the floor. I picked up another. And another. And I'd just found a repeat copy of Great Expectations when Maggie came into the library.

"I'm okay," she told me before I could say anything. "I don't want to talk about it. And no, I don't want you to break Robby's jaw or any other part of his body for me. I can handle him myself, okay?"

"Okay," I answered. I could live with that. For now.

"And same goes for Andrew."

I frowned. "Hell no. I can't make any promises with Andrew. He's at the top of my shit-list and not just because of you. Anyway, want to go watch some old 80's movies, eat ice cream, and pretend our problems don't exist?"

"Yes," she muttered, seeming relieved that I'd asked her to do regular stuff today.

"Okay. Good. I've got to make a quick phone call to Mary Ann at the Pro Shop. I was supposed to golf with Clara this morning. Let me do that and then we can watch a movie."

She gave me a small smile and I pulled out my phone. It was already after eleven and it killed me to have to cancel on Clara. Absolutely killed me. She wouldn't even know I was cancelling on her and it still bugged me. But I felt like Maggie needed me a little more in this moment. I made the quick call to Mary Ann, while Maggie left to go get some snacks ready for our movie. Watching old 80's movies was kind of our thing. I wanted it to be my thing with Clara too—like it had been when we were all younger.

After I got off the phone, I absentmindedly flipped through the copy of Great Expectations I still held in my hand. Not expecting to find anything, since I was beginning to think that clover was lost forever, I froze when I saw something dark green tucked inside a page.

The clover.

It was the clover. It was still intact.

And if that wasn't a giant, neon sign that Clara and I were supposed to be together, I didn't know what was.

CHAPTER 14:

Dinner was supposed to be happening at six at the Ryder's house. It was five after six. I laid across the Ryder's couch, while Maggie sat the back patio table for dinner and Reed finished grilling the lobster tails he'd cooked for tonight. I'm not sure why he wanted us all to have dinner together—including me—but that's what was about to happen.

Clara had been doing her golf lesson thing all day long and now that six was finally here, I felt so on-edge that I wanted to scream. The problem was…I didn't know where I stood with her. Sure, we'd kissed in the airport this morning—dramatically, like she was sending me off to war or something. But what would happen when she showed up at her house and found me in it? For all I knew, she still thought I was in New York. For all I knew, that was where she wanted me to stay.

But I wasn't in New York. I was here because Clara was here. And if she really was as serious about us as she'd appeared to be last night and this morning then it wouldn't be an issue that I'd taken liberties, showing up at her house.

Right? Right.

The sound of the front door opening caused my screwed up brain to focus. Clara was here.

"Hey guys, I'm home," she called out to the house. Since the sliding glass door that lead out to the back patio was closed, Reed and Maggie didn't hear Clara. I stood up, waiting for her to walk in and find me.

But she didn't notice me in the living room. Instead, she walked into the kitchen, dumping her purse onto the counter. She stared across the room, looking outside at her family.

God, she was breathtaking. She wore gym clothes—a bright yellow tank top and pants that fit her ass like a glove. Her purple hair hung over one of her shoulders. Simply unable to resist the girl, I went toward her. Not even my own fears and insecurities could stop what was about to happen next.

I snuck up behind her, wrapping my arms around her waist and pulling her body against my own. Instantly she leaned back against my chest, a small moan escaping her lips. Bliss ran through me as she let me touch her.

I could tell she'd had an exhausting day. Neither of us had slept much last night, and Clara had been in the hot Virginia sun all day. But for the way she relaxed into me, it told me everything I needed to know. She was happy I was here. She didn't ask the details of when I'd gotten home to Blue Creek. She only rested her head back against my shoulder. An open invitation for me to kiss her neck.

She smelled like the sun as I planted a trail of kisses over her bare shoulder and across her neck. "Hi, killer," I whispered. "You're like fucking nirvana for sore eyes." My hands slipped up and down her waist, exploring and needing to touch as much of her as possible. "I didn't know I could miss you so much after only a few hours, and I love that I can touch you like this." My touch grew bolder and I moved my hands over her chest. Hell, from the way she was arching into me it felt like this was exactly what she wanted me to do. I gently squeezed and caressed her breasts above her shirt. "Tell me I'm a pervert and I have to stop. Tell me and I will."

She told me nothing. So stopping was the furthest thing from my mind.

And then, as if I wasn't turned on enough and straining painfully in the confines of my pants, she pressed into me more. "Hmm," she murmured, her voice throaty, as she felt my erection pushing against her ass.

"Dammit. Tell me now, Clara," I demanded.

And when no words came from her mouth still, I took that as my green light.

"Okay then. I gave you fair warning. Remember that."

My hands continued their exploration. Her breathing turned heavy and choppy. And then, partly to see if I could and partly because I couldn't stop myself, I moved one of my hands inside her shirt. My fingers grazed over her tight, little nipple.

Clara shivered against me.

Jesus Christ.

And then she steadied herself by placing both hands on the counter in front of us. Shit. This was hot. My body was on fire. If her family wasn't right outside I'd be stripping her naked and having my way with her right this moment, right against this counter. The best part was the way Clara reacted to my touch. She wanted me as bad as I wanted her.

That reminded me that her family was in eye-shot. I quickly moved her a few feet to the left so we were out of view. I knew I didn't have long with her, but I wasn't ready for this small moment to be over yet either. So in a move that was a remnant of the old me, the pre-celibate me, I pushed that yellow tank top of hers down, completely exposing her breasts to the kitchen. My fingers grazed over her sensitive flesh. Her nipples were so hard, despite the fact that it wasn't cold at all in the kitchen.

"You have the most perfect tits," I whispered. "I've been fantasizing about touching them since we were twelve years old." Taking her waist in my hands, I turned her around to face me. I even took a small step back so I could better see her. Her naked chest was right there, perfect and all for me. I couldn't breathe. I couldn't really think. And as much as I wanted to study her body. I couldn't take my eyes off her eyes. I couldn't look away from the way she was staring back at me—so trusting, so enamored.

"You're beautiful," I whispered, kissing her cheek. Then I pulled her tank top back up so that it once again covered her chest. "Too beautiful."

My eyes left hers. And I felt my face flush. Seeing her partially naked and seeing the way she'd completely let me look at her, not to mention touch her, was too damn much. Moving across the kitchen, breathing a little too heavily, I gripped the edge of the counter and tried to regain my composure. Her confidence was so sexy it was crippling.

"Leo. You're—" she started to say, but never finished her thought because Reed and Maggie walked into the kitchen.

Fuck. I'd forgotten they existed. Good thing everything had stopped between Clara when it did or they would have found her with her shirt down. I think Clara realized this too—because she had the biggest, cheesiest, most adorable grin plastered on her face.

"There you are," Reed said to her. "Honey, I'm sure you're tired. Dinner's almost ready, but why don't you go shower first? Oh, and there is aloe under my sink. You're a little sunburned."

I don't think she was as sunburned as Reed thought. I'm pretty sure her cheeks were red on account of me. Oh well, I wasn't about to correct him. Let him think she was red from a sunburn.

"Okay." Clara nodded, avoiding my gaze.

"Why are you smiling like that?" Maggie asked her, noticing something was up between us.

"I'm having a good day," Clara answered and then she hurried from the room.

"Hmm," Reed muttered. "Maybe she doesn't hate golf as much as she pretends to." Then he grabbed the biggest ceramic platter I'd ever seen, tucking it under one arm, and with his other free hand he grabbed his special butter-lemon sauce that was for the lobster. Maggie helped him open the sliding glass door.

I flipped open the fully-stocked fridge. “Want a water?” I asked Maggie.

“Sure.”

I handed her one, then grabbed one for myself and one for Clara. We joined Reed out on the back patio. He took his lobster tails off the grill and plated them. Then he sat down in his usual spot at the head of the table, while Maggie sat beside him where she always did. Typically, if I was joining the Ryder family for dinner, I would have sat beside Maggie. It was what was expected of me and what I always did. But I sat in the seat beside Clara’s usual seat. In fact—I was damn sick of always doing what everyone expected.

A moment later, Clara came rushing outside with her long hair still damp and hanging down over her shoulders. She wore a similar outfit to the one she’d been in a few minutes ago. Except her tank top was pink this time. It clashed with her hair, but she didn’t seem to mind or care as she gave me a quick smile. She took the seat next to mine like it wasn't weird that I’d chosen to sit beside her instead of beside Maggie.

And, for being the smaller twin, the girl always had a giant appetite. Tonight was no different. She started loading food onto her plate like she was a two-hundred pound man. Once she finished, she sat there waiting because Reed had a strict rule about saying prayer before eating. When she noticed everyone staring at her she explained, “I'm so hungry I could eat this table. I didn't have breakfast or lunch. And Mary Ann is such a ‘you-know-what’ that she wouldn't even let me borrow a dollar to hit up the vending machine. I guess I should start carrying cash around like you always say, Dad.”

I guess, for once, I was right. Mary Ann was a bitch.

“You should have called me,” I told her. “I would have brought you something.”

“I didn't know you were back in Blue Creek until...” Clara paused, her voice nearly whispering, “Until a few minutes ago.”

“Okay then.” I grabbed Clara's hand in mine, locking our fingers, and then reached across the table for Maggie’s. She gave me the oddest look and then hesitantly took my hand. Then I glanced in Reed’s direction, staring at him impatiently. “Say the prayer, Reed. Please. So she can eat already.”

Reed’s mouth was hanging open, and it appeared I’d rendered him speechless. I’m not exactly sure why he was so shocked. I thought I’d made it perfectly clear this morning that Clara and I were more than enemies now. Maybe seeing it first hand, seeing us together in person, was weird for him. It was still a little weird for me too. But whatever. He needed to get used to it.

After a few moments of sitting frozen in place, Reed swallowed hard and then completed the circle before saying the blessing.

“So,” Clara started, “I gave Old Man Sinclair golf lessons today and I found out he turns eighty-three this weekend. You should throw a party for him, Dad. I mean, he's been a member forever and you're always looking for excuses to throw parties. What do you think?”

Her dad nodded. “That sounds wonderful. I have my tournament in Miami this weekend, but I can set everything up with Darlene, the event planner. Those things practically run themselves anyway. What a great idea, honey. Would you like to host it?”

Clara shrugged, while taking another giant bite of lobster. “Um, okay. I guess I could do that.”

“You don't have to do anything other than show up,” Reed said.

"That's all I do when I host."

All of a sudden, totally out of character, Maggie dropped her fork to her plate dramatically. The clinking sound got everyone's attention. "I had to work for you Saturday morning, Clara," she snapped at her sister. "You called out and the restaurant was short-staffed and I worked for you. You're welcome. It would have been nice to run away to New York with Leo for the weekend, but some of us are mature enough to handle our responsibilities."

What the hell was her problem? I glared across the table at Maggie, wondering from where all of her sudden rage was coming. So much for Clara's plan to try to smooth some of their sister-hate over. Judging by this outburst, I'd say they were still mortal enemies.

"And," Maggie continued on, "you could have killed Leo! Not to mention, the extra work you created for the landscaping staff, thanks to your joyriding. Do you even think?"

"Maggie," Reed groaned, stopping her. "We could sit here and go over every little thing Clara did wrong this weekend or we could have a nice family dinner. It's not often that we all get to sit down together like this."

Immediately Maggie stood to her feet. "I'm sorry, guys, I'm feeling sick," she announced, obviously lying. "I ate way too much ice cream earlier with Leo. This dinner looks delicious, Dad, but I really need to go lie down." And with those parting words, she left the patio and hurried inside.

Well, that was weird.

"Leo, actually, would you please go and get Maggie for me?" Reed asked. "I called this family dinner tonight with a purpose and I need all three of you present for what has to be said."

That sounded rather ominous.

Giving Clara a quick glance, I stood and followed in the direction

Maggie had gone. Inside, I raced up the carpeted stairs toward the second level. I had to pass Clara's room to get to Maggie's. I'd never—at least not since we were much younger—been in Clara's room. And as I passed I peaked inside, taking in all her posters and random artsy stuff, I was excited over the possibilities of finally getting to know the Clara I'd always been able to watch only from afar.

But unfortunately now wasn't the time for that, and I went for Maggie's pink room instead.

She sat on the edge of her bed, hugging a pillow tight to her chest.

"Hey," I said, inching into her room

"Hey," she replied, giving me a small smile.

"Your dad wants you back downstairs. He has something he needs to tell us all."

She frowned.

"Are you okay, Maggie?" I asked. "You've been a little off all day. Are you sure you're okay with Clara and I being together? I know it's happening fast, but it's going to be permanent…so I need you to be okay with this."

She sighed. "I just need time, Leo. I've always had you all to myself and now…suddenly…I don't."

The muscles in my jaw tightened and I slowly nodded. "Just so you know, no matter what, nothing could ever change *our* friendship. You're the only thing in my crazy life that has ever been a fucking constant. Nothing will ever change that." Jesus. I never realized dating Clara might hurt Maggie. I rubbed my hands through my hair. "So would you please come back downstairs? You and Clara have your issues—I get that—but I'd really like you to come finish dinner with us."

"I thought Dad needed me downstairs."

"He does. But I'd like you down there too."

My words must have been reassuring. Because Maggie dropped the pillow and walked with me downstairs. Who the hell knows what Reed had to say to all three of us, but it had better not be anything along the lines of Clara not being allowed to date me. The shit would hit the fan if he was about to say I couldn't be with her.

* * *

"Have a seat," Reed said as Maggie and I came back outside, "We have something to discuss."

Judging by the way his eyes were too serious and his voice too stern, my stomach immediately started to churn. Maggie sat down at once, saying nothing. It took me an extra moment, but I decided to sit, too. In my seat. By Clara. Adrenaline started rushing through my veins, making me feel shaky.

"It's about Dean," Dad stated.

Hell, not what I was expecting. I'm glad we weren't going to discuss my relationship with Clara, but I certainly didn't feel relieved. The opposite actually. "Motherfucker," I swore. Hardly appropriate for the dinner table but it had to be said. "His lurking ass is really starting to piss me off. Did Maggie tell you how he showed up on my doorstep this morning like a complete stalker? Reed, you need to tell him to get out of our lives. He's starting to screw with Maggie's head. Hell, he's starting to screw with my head."

"He's not screwing with my head," Maggie defended. "I'm just fine."

I groaned. Maggie was protecting him now? Case and point.

"By fine," I said to her, "you mean he's wormed his way back into your life without explanation of where he's been for the last six years? Maybe you've forgotten the way things went down, Mags, but I haven't. That bastard made you promises on top of promises and he never kept one of them. Now he's suddenly back and you're *fine*. Well, I'm not fucking fine."

Shit. I didn't realize how mad I was about Robby's reappearance until this very moment.

"This is my life and you need to let me handle it, Leo," Maggie whined. "I get that you're trying to protect me, but I really can handle this. I'm fine with him coming back to Blue Creek. He's been nice to me."

Reed nodded in agreement with Maggie. "She's right. Dean's a good man. He hasn't had an easy life, but I trust that he's just trying to do right by what he knows. Anyway, it's not Dean I wanted to discuss. This is about his daughter, Valerie."

"Who the hell is Dean?" Clara snapped, cutting him off before he could say anymore.

"Robby," we all answered in unison.

It occurred to me that Clara hadn't heard about her ex-stepbrother's new name. I leaned back in my seat and tilted closer to her. "Dean is Robby," I explained, feeling somehow calmer talking with her in this moment. "He changed his name, tricked Maggie into bringing him as her date to the gala the other night when she didn't recognize him, and now he's being secretive as hell."

Maggie again jumped to Dean's defense. "He didn't trick me!"

"Robby has a daughter?" Clara asked, not seeming to care about the rest of the drama. "How old?"

"Five," Reed answered.

"Oh," she breathed. "This is incredible. Crazy—but incredible."

A hint of a smile appeared on Reed's face. "I think so too."

"What's incredible?" Maggie asked, confused. She looked from Clara to Reed. "Daddy?"

"Oh, that's just great," I grumbled, realizing exactly what Reed and now Clara seemed to be thinking. "Reed thinks Robby's *daughter* might be his daughter."

Robby and his gold-digging mother, Monica, left Blue Creek, and all of us, roughly six years ago. And if Robby's daughter was five years old, that meant he would have had to have knocked someone up very soon after they'd left. So either it had happened like that. Or someone had knocked up flaky Monica and Robby was caring for her child now. Was that someone Reed?

I guess anything was possible.

"It's mere speculation," Reed mused. "The only thing I am basing this on is the girl's age."

Maggie's face held little emotion as she spoke. "She looks so much like Robby. She has his dark hair and his eyes. Even his height. But I guess it could be possible...it would mean..." She swallowed hard. "It might mean that Robby never broke any of his promises to me. And having her as a sister would be kind of wonderful. She's really sweet. What are you going to do about it, Dad?"

"Nothing." Reed shrugged. "There's nothing I can do right now."

I choked on a big gulp of air. *What? Why would he even be speculating if he didn't plan on doing anything?* "The hell you can't! You can call your lawyer. You can demand a paternity test. If it turns out she is your kid, Reed, then you can fight for custody. Nothing, my ass."

"No," he urged, "I can't do any of that. If Monica had custody of the girl, then I would do everything in my power to fight for her. But—and this is what I was trying to say before—Dean is a good man. His name change was about his father, nothing else. Now it's his story to tell so I won't go into the details, but it's clear he's had a lot on his plate over the last six years and good reasons for not getting here sooner. Now he's back in Blue Creek and I get the impression that he's back because he wants to make things right. We have to have faith in him and wait this out."

Reed wanted to let Robby reveal everything in his own time. But it was because of Reed's *good faith* that Robby's scheming con-artist of a mother took a lot of his money in a messy divorce the first time around. Was Robby just as conniving as his mother? I'd say...probably.

Reed and I continued to argue. Back and forth, we debated on the possibilities and what should be done.

"Look," Clara suddenly interrupted. "I'm overjoyed at the possibility of having another sister," she told everyone. "Really, I am. Best news ever. But I have to agree with Leo on this one. We have to do *something*."

I shot Clara a look. Holy shit, did she just agree with me? We were damn good at arguing, but it was such a change to be agreeing about something that it nearly knocked me out of my chair. And, actually, it felt really nice knowing she had my back. My whole body physically seemed to relax because of it. I caught her hand under the table and gently squeezed. It might have been only a couple words she'd given me, but they meant everything to me.

"If you didn't want to take any action," I started, my voice ten times calmer now, "then you shouldn't have included me in this conversation. I'm pissed and you're indifferent and there's nothing I can do about it."

Reed, who hadn't raised his voice once or faltered from his calm demeanor throughout our whole conversation, looked hurt by my words. "I included *all of you* in this conversation because *all of you* are my family. You too, Leo. And when the shit hits the fan, if you can't turn to your family, then who can you turn to? Finding out I might have another child is not an easy pill to swallow. I'm not indifferent—I'm pissed too. I'm angry and sad that I missed the first five years of this girl's life, but I'm trying my best to stay calm. I'm trying to decide what the best thing is for us and for Valerie."

"Okay then," I said, finally admitting defeat. "Can I at least call my private detective and see if he can dig up anything on Monica or Robby?"

"Sure. That's a good idea."

"I need to catch my breath," Maggie announced as she stood to her feet. "I'm going to go for a drive. I might stay the night in Blacksburg if I make it all the way up there. All this...it's just a lot to take in—"

Ding dong. The front door bell was barely audible on the back deck, but Maggie stopped speaking instantly and her face paled at the sound.

I think we were all thinking the same thing. *Shit, was it Robby?*

"All three of you, I want you to promise me right now—not a word of this," Reed whispered. "I mean it. If that's Dean at the door, then not a word. I need time to figure out exactly what I want to do and he can't know that we know."

Ding dong. Ding dong. Ding dong.

"Man, someone is sure persistent. I'll go get it," Clara offered, jumping up from her seat.

I handed Maggie my half-full water bottle…because she looked like she needed some water. A minute or two passed and Clara didn't return. "Hell," I thought aloud, "I'm going to go check and see if it's him." I stood.

Maggie stood too. "Yeah, me too."

"I'll wait here," Reed said, finally taking a bite of his untouched food.

Maggie and I hurried through the house. She started to say something to me, but as we neared the front door, I motioned for her to be quiet.

It wasn't Robby on the porch with Clara.

It was Andrew Fucking Wellington.

CHAPTER 15:

Wanting to strangle Andrew Wellington until his beady little eyes popped out of his head but wanting to hear what Clara might say to him a little bit more, I ducked down next to the front the door. Maggie kneeled beside me.

"He keeps showing up wanting Clara," Maggie whispered. "Last time he came by with flowers! He never did that for me."

Clara had left the door cracked and I motioned for Maggie to be quiet again. I desperately needed to hear whatever was being said out on that porch.

"Are you here for a reason?" Clara's voice asked impatiently on the other side of the door. I couldn't see her, but I could picture the bored, indifferent look on her face that went along with that voice. She used to use it on me all the time. "My family is kind of in the middle of something and—"

Something cut off her words. Because I heard nothing next. Inching forward, both Maggie and I peeked through the crack in the door. Fuckface was kissing Clara. Forcefully. I nearly flung myself out that door. But as immediately as he must have forced himself on her, Clara pushed at his chest and said, "Sorry, Andrew. You can't kiss me. I fucked Leo."

I sucked in a sharp breath.

Maggie let out a small gasp.

Clara said those untrue words and I hardly knew what to think. But, nonetheless, they were effective words. Andrew let her go immediately, stepping backward off the porch. Standing in the grass, he bent over with his hands on his knees and his face wrinkled in pain.

"Once?" he coughed out.

"No. Repeatedly," Clara said, lying once more.

She was cold as ice as she spoke too. Emotionless. Heartless. I still didn't know what to make of it all.

Andrew moaned, clutching one hand to his chest. It took him several long seconds to compose himself. I swear to God, I think he was going to vomit. But when he finally did glance up at Clara, my heart almost broke for him. Almost. Not quite. And then I realized…everything that was happening now had been Clara's plan all along.

She wanted to hurt Andrew—the same way he'd hurt her sister. He'd fallen in love with her and now she was tossing him aside like yesterday's garbage. I wasn't sure if I was impressed or deathly afraid. If Clara hurt me like that…I doubt I'd ever recover.

"I went away with him to New York for the weekend and it just happened," she explained to him, her voice turning a little gentler now.

He nodded and slowly straightened back up. "Are you going to keep fucking him?" Andrew bit out.

"Yes," she responded, a little breathless. "We're together now. Like *together* together."

Andrew groaned. "Then you should know he does this sort of thing all the time."

"What sort of thing?"

"Do you really think you're the first girl he's whisked away on his private jet and put up in one of his fancy park suites in Manhattan? You're a pretty toy, Clara, but for the kid who has everything money can buy, there will always be a prettier toy out there. And when Leo gets bored—like he always does—where will that leave you?"

My breath became trapped in my lungs. Clara and I were barely together and obviously we'd had no opportunities to discuss our past relationships. But if Andrew was going under then it was apparent he wanted to take me down with him. His words made my heart feel like it was being squeezed through a vice. I finally had Clara looking at me the way I'd always wanted her to look at me—and now I had to deal with this.

Because, unfortunately, Andrew's words about my past were the absolute truth. Before that night on that balcony, I often used my money, good looks, and personal jet to trick women into sleeping with me. I'd spend each weekend lavishly showering a different girl with gifts, screwing her brains out, and then come Monday I'd get rid of her the way Clara was getting rid of Andrew.

I hated Andrew. But I was no better than him.

And then, like the cherry on top of a shit Sunday, Andrew gave Clara a hug. It was an honest-to-goodness genuine hug. I could do nothing but stand there and watch it happen. She didn't return his gesture, but she didn't push him away either.

"Leo's not good enough for you," he told her. "He's not good enough for anyone. Don't let him into your heart because he will break it the first chance he gets." He let his arms fall away from the girl I feared was no longer mine and then he started walking off toward his car.

"You're wrong," she shouted before Andrew could leave. "Leo's good. Maybe some of the stuff he does isn't so good, but he's good. He would never hurt me."

What? I couldn't believe she'd told him that after finding out about my repulsive past behavior. Andrew disappeared into his car and drove away, and the very moment he was gone I pushed open the front door and stepped outside to confront Clara. She shouldn't have called me good. It somehow hit a cord deep inside me.

"You mean that?" I asked her.

She shrieked in surprise and whipped around to find me standing on the porch behind her. Jesus Christ. Instead of appearing angry with me, she stared up at me…as if she was searching for *my* acceptance. As if she were afraid I might be angry with her for what just transpired between her and Andrew. Dammit. Just when I thought I couldn't possibly love her anymore, I fell for the girl all over again.

Nervous as hell, I rubbed a hand over the back of my neck.

"How much of that did you hear?" she demanded.

"Everything. Maggie and I heard everything."

The front door opened wider, revealing Maggie.

"Why did you tell him we slept together when we haven't?" I asked.

Her face flushed a deep shade of red. "I don't know. I wanted to hurt him. Did Maggie tell you that he cheated on her? When he confessed he liked me a couple of weeks ago, that's when I came up with the idea to fake-date him. I thought I could use his feelings against him—make him fall hard and then crush him the first chance I got. Seemed like now or never," she explained, shrugging her shoulders.

I gave her a small smile. "Well, I personally enjoyed seeing Andrew bent over, dry-heaving on your front lawn."

Maggie giggled. "Classic."

"You guys saw that?"

"We were watching from inside," Maggie answered. "Next time just kick him in the balls. It will have the same effect and get the job done quicker."

Despite everything, Clara laughed.

"You're ruthless, killer," I told her, smiling widely now, "and very deserving of that nickname."

"Well," Maggie interrupting, probably sensing that Clara and I needed some time alone, "I'm still going for a drive, so I better go before it gets dark." Then she hugged Clara. Of all things, she hugged Clara. "Thanks for getting even with Andrew for me. You're braver than I am," she said to her sister and walked off toward the garage.

"Are you mad about what I told Andrew?" she asked, now that we were alone.

God, how could she even ask me that? After the things Andrew told her…she was somehow seeking *my* approval. Crossing my arms tightly over my chest, I moved to lean against the porch railing.

"No. I don't care if you tell the whole world that we slept together," I joked. But I couldn't even play off my feelings with my normal cockiness, so I went for the truth instead. "I'm hoping one day it might be the truth. But you need to know...some of the stuff Andrew said about me is true. I *have* taken other girls for weekends away in my jet. Not because I liked them, but because I wanted to get them in bed. I haven't done that sort of thing for a while now, but that doesn't excuse it." I sighed heavily. "Because I'm crazy about *you.* This isn't the time or the place I wanted to say this, but you need to know...I'm in love with you, Clara, I always have been."

* * *

"What?" The word burst from Clara's mouth. She turned away from me and sat down onto the concrete steps of her front porch.

"I love you," I repeated. Now that I'd said those three little words, there was no longer any need to hide anything.

"Yeah, I heard that part already," she groaned. "So, last summer when I called you 'gay' and you called me a 'lesbian'—you were secretly in love with me the whole time?"

"Yes."

"At my graduation party, when you called me 'ridiculous' and said I was a baby for getting into that fight with Dad, telling him I never wanted to play stupid golf again—you secretly loved me then too?"

"You *were* being ridiculous and childish. Everyone knows how much you love golf. But yes, then too."

"And when—"

"Yes, Clara. Yes, every single moment, good or bad, I've loved you."

"Why?" she demanded, glancing over her shoulder, her eyes tentatively finding mine. She had tears in her eyes. And it hurt that she'd even question why I'd loved her. Of course I loved her. "Why?" she repeated. "Why me? I don't understand."

"I don't understand it either," I said and then quickly shook my head before adding, "No, that's not true. I understand it perfectly." Moving across the porch, I sat down beside her on the steps. Desperate to touch her somehow, I reached out and intertwined one of my hands with one of hers. Her whole body tensed and I believe her hands were trembling. But hell, my hands may have been shaking as well.

She stared down at our joined hands, unwilling or unable to meet her eyes, as I spoke.

"I love you because you say and do whatever the hell you feel," I told her. "You aren't afraid to call me on my shit and tell me when I'm being an asshole. You look at life differently than anyone I've ever met—like it's a gift and you can't get enough. You don't make friends easily, but when you do, you're the most loyal person I know. You can be incredibly thoughtful yet unbelievably stubborn, and I love both of those sides of you. And when we're in the same room...I can't take my eyes off of you. I always want to be near you and hear what you have to say, even if it only leads to us fighting."

A small sob left Clara's lips. Her gaze left our hands and our eyes met.

My free hand cupped her beautiful pink cheek as I finished what I needed to say, "I care about you so much it hurts. I want this to work between us. I've never wanted anything more."

Her eyes drifted closed and she leaned into my touch. It was in this moment that I knew I had Clara's heart. I don't know if it's something I'd had all along or if I won her over that very moment, but I could feel my love returned in this one small gesture. It was as if I'd been searching for something that was lost my entire life and had suddenly found it.

I dipped my head closer to hers, brushing my lips against her shoulder.

"Um." She swallowed and opened her eyes. "What did you mean when you said you haven't done 'that sort of thing' for a while? You haven't taken girls to different destinations or you haven't…uh, dated?" Her cheeks blushed bright red as she asked this.

"Both. I lost myself for a long time to drugs and drinking and girls, but you saved me. Without even knowing it, you helped pull me out of the dark. That night freshman year, when I fell off that balcony in The Village, a lot of shitty things had been running through my head. Then you appeared and it reminded me of how crazy I'd always been about you. It gave me hope when I needed it more than ever. And since that night, I've been working at being better. I'm not sure I'm 'good' like you told Andrew, but I'm trying. And no, I haven't dated since then. I've been all yours, even if you didn't know it. Always yours. Do you remember sitting with me after I fell that night?"

She took a deep breath, closing her eyes for a small moment—as if she was remembering the very moment that meant everything to me. When she opened her eyes, she slowly nodded.

"A few minutes with you was all I needed and suddenly nothing seemed so bad anymore. So, even if nothing comes from this—if it all ends tonight—then at least you finally know how I feel. Either way, I'm always going to be here and I'm always going to love you. It's not something I can stop. Trust me, I've tried. But like I said when I kissed you in the Alligator Lounge, I sure as hell don't want to fight my feelings anymore." I stood to my feet, my hands moving to my pockets.

I'd just pulled out all the stops—said everything I felt inside my chest. I needed her to say something in return.

"Leo, I—" she started.

Totally interrupting the moment, Reed came out the front door and joined us on the porch. "Oh, there you kids are." His eyes shifted back and forth between us—like he knew he'd just killed our moment. I loved him, but hated him for his timing.

"Did you need something, Dad?" Clara asked impatiently.

"Yeah," he answered. "I called Ed over at Ed's Heads Salon. He happened to be there late today and said you could come over. You need to leave now though. He won't wait around forever."

No! I loved her purple hair.

"Fine, Dad," she grunted.

What the hell? Was she not even going to fight him on this? She fought him on everything else.

"And Leo," Reed said, motioning for me to follow him. "Come inside and tell me more about that private detective you know."

Reed disappeared through the front door, fully expecting me to follow behind immediately.

Fuck that.

"I better go," Clara said. "He's going to harass me until I change my hair."

I frowned. "I like the purple."

“Me too. But you know how it is, all about appearances around here…”

“Oh, believe me, I know.” I knew a little too well. “If you want…you can come over to my place after. I'll be around,” I said, feeling so uncharacteristically unsure of myself.

She nodded, surprising me by brushing a quick kiss against my lips, and then she hurried for the garage.

CHAPTER 16:

My father called me…yelling. The man had a frosty, mean, stoic way about him, but he never yelled. Or I guess I should say, he *rarely* yelled. It had taken him a few hours to notice that I wasn't in the correct city and that I wasn't doing the job I was supposed to be doing. He used words like disgrace, disappointment, unworthy—all of it trying to rattle me. And it very nearly worked.

My name and my legacy meant a lot to me. And as much as I would have loved to disappoint my father on purpose, to rub his own bullshit back in his face, I also had some jacked-up need to please him.

"I'm in fucking Blue Creek, Virginia," I told him over the phone. "It's not like I'm on a month-long drinking binge in Mexico! Christ, I never take time off. I'll be back soon enough. Maybe in a week." *God, Clara's hair appointment was taking forever.* I wished she was here to distract me away from everything else in my life.

"A week! I'd rather you be in Mexico. Don't be ungrateful, Leonardo. Just get back here."

I sighed. "I can't."

"What do you mean *you can't?* Take the jet."

Even if I tried to explain that I was following my heart for once in my damn life, I don't think he would have understood. Or he'd call me stupid and naïve for it. Maybe I was stupid and naïve. But still…I wasn't about to leave just because he told me to.

"Have you ever wanted something so much that nothing else seems to matter?" I asked him, genuinely curious as to how he might answer. "Something you'd do almost anything for?"

"Yes," he answered quickly. "I want your grandfather to retire so that I can take over this company. But wishful thinking is for the weak and the poor. Neither of which are we. You can have a week to do whatever you need to do, Leo. Then come home."

I gritted my teeth. "Fine."

"Fine," he answered.

Then we both hung up.

Defeated and tired, I plopped down on the sofa in my den. Before my father had called, I'd been sorting through junk in this room—figuring out what I wanted to keep and what I wanted to get rid of. I'd been meaning to clear out and renovate this house ever since I bought it from him. But it occurred to me now…the reason none of that had been done was because I was never in Blue Creek long enough to do it.

At some point after that thrilling phone conversation, I must have fallen asleep on that uncomfortable sofa in the den. Clara woke me. My eyes opened and I found her hovering over me in the darkened room. The sun had set during my cat-nap.

No words were exchanged, but she reached out her hand. I took it. She tugged, expecting me to follow her wherever. And so I followed her. She led me around piles of clutter and junk, toward the staircase. She wanted me upstairs.

Each step upward felt like a mile and my heart drummed so hard it beat in my ears. My bedroom sat directly off the top of the stairs and it was clear that was exactly where she was leading me. Even a blind person could have sensed Clara's motives in this moment. A hell of a lot more than kissing was about to happen next.

Once inside my room with the door shut firmly behind us, Clara planted both of her hands on my chest and gave me a small shove toward my bed. I didn't budge for her, and when she tried a second shove, I caught her wrists against my chest. Clara stuck her lip out and gave me a small pout.

"What are you doing?" I whispered.

"You," she said, taking a deep breath.

Fuck me. Was she serious?

I wanted to push her down onto my bed, strip her naked, and do things to her I'd always dreamt of doing to her. But I didn't want to jeopardize anything either. "I don't want to rush this," I explained.

She tried to wiggle her hands free from where I still clutched them tightly to my chest. I couldn't let her go. Because if I did then I wasn't sure what would happen next.

"Who cares if we rush this?" she asked softly, as if she were trying to put all my nerves at ease. "I don't. You shouldn't either. I'm not ready to say certain words out loud, but I can give you something else. I can show you how I'm feeling. Please, Leo. Let me show you. You told me on the subway to stop over-thinking and now you're doing the same exact thing. So, stop it."

How could I argue with that? I couldn't. I couldn't do a damn thing but let her pull free from my grip. She wanted me. It was painfully obvious. And there was no stopping a determined Clara.

Standing on her toes, she pressed her lips to mine and kissed me. I went through the motions of returning her kiss, but to be completely honest, I was scared out of my damn mind. It had been over two years since I'd last had sex. What if I messed something up? Or forgot how to do it right? Not to mention, I don't think I'd ever once had sober sex. Shit, what if I ruined this by not living up to her expectations? Because in the past, girls always had high expectations of my sexual abilities. I was confident and cocky with clothes on—they expected me to be even more so without them.

One of her hands moved under my shirt, her fingers tracing over my abs. Her breathing turned heavy as she did this—as if merely touching my stomach was turning the girl on. Her eyes glanced shyly up at mine. Then she grabbed the edges of my shirt and surprised the hell out of me by yanking it up over my head.

Slow down, Clara, I thought. But my body wasn't in tune with my head anymore. I'd grown dangerously hard, letting Clara do whatever she wanted with me. I couldn't find the words or the strength to stop her. Watching her was fun and exciting. How far would she go with this? I stood perfectly still because a big part of me wanted to find out.

Next she went for my belt buckle, unhooking it, and then my shorts. My clothing dropped unceremoniously to the ground, *leaving nothing left!* And I'd forgotten underwear this morning…so yeah, I was naked.

Clara's eyes traced up and down my naked form. She studied me…my tattoos, my arms, my chest, my abs…even my dick. And suddenly I grew angry.

The thing about picking up girls, flying them to New York, and screwing them in my penthouse suite…the thing was…they all were using *me* just as much as I used them. And my heart broke because it seemed Clara was about to do the same exact thing. On the porch I'd been so confident of her feelings—knowing with all my heart that she felt what I felt. Suddenly that confidence shattered. And it pissed me the hell off.

She dropped to her knees. All her clothes were still on for fuck's sake. She reached out and took me in her hand. My mind was undergoing an internal battle. Because having Clara touch me and stare up at me from her knees was sexy as hell. I was desperate to see what she'd do next. And that desperation trumped the sense of dread in my chest.

Her hand moved carefully over my skin, stroking toward the base of my length and then back toward the tip. Her fingers traced with the lightest of touches. A groan slipped from my throat. It sounded guttural and primitive. And I couldn't help it. I dropped my head back, my mouth falling open, succumbing to Clara. Fine. If she wanted to have her way with me then I suppose I'd let her. What the fuck ever. I'd enjoy the moment and go to war with her later. So be it.

My eyes drifted closed as I relished the feel of her hand. But they snapped open in the very next moment…because her mouth replaced her hand.

"Whoa, killer. You don't have to do anything you don't...."

My sentence went unfinished. I couldn't get the rest of my words out because she didn't let me. She dug her fingernails into my ass and sucked me deeper into her mouth. I said every curse word known to man, knotted my fingers through her hair, and even started moving my hips to match her rhythm…was it shaky? Her eyes flickered up to mine and that was when it occurred to me—Clara didn't have a clue what she was doing. Her tongue moved too fast; her pressure was too light; her confidence seemed to be forced. God, my dick was in her mouth, so obviously I enjoyed the view and the feel of her mouth immensely. But was this her first time giving head? Damn, what if it was? What if she was a virgin too?

From the way she stared up at me, looking for *my* approval, I think I'd just figured her out.

Holy shit.

Just as Clara had started to find a decent rhythm, I moved myself out of her mouth, grabbed the sides of her arms, and pulled her fully clothed body up against my naked one. And I kissed her. I kissed her with all the passion that was growing and expanding inside my chest. It had now become clear to me that she *was* inexperienced. How could I not see this before?

I couldn't help but fall a little deeper in love with her. Shivers shot through my heart. I'd seen the intensity and the care in her eyes earlier when we'd sat on her porch. And I felt it now in her kiss. She didn't want to just use me for my body like I'd feared minutes before. Someone without experience wouldn't do that. And if she really was a virgin…then knowing that she wanted to give it up to *me*...well, that made my heart swell with pride, and an arrogance I'd been missing for quite some time returned.

I kissed her until we were both completely breathless. I rested my forehead against her forehead and stared fiercely into her pretty gray eyes. A smile came to my lips. If Clara wanted me then she was going to get me.

"I need to be inside you," I whispered in a husky growl. I pushed gently at her shoulders, so that she fell backward onto my unmade bed. Clara stared back at me, challenging me.

The first things that I had to get rid of were her shoes and socks. Then her pants went next. Jesus Christ, rational thought had left me and I hardly cared. Sex or no sex, I'd still feel the same way about her tomorrow. The sex would only magnify everything, so it suddenly became my only focus.

Now that those annoying articles of clothing were out of the way, my pace slowed because I didn't want her first time—*still assuming this was her first time*—to be rushed in anyway. I inched the fabric of her tank top upward, planting a trail of kisses and little licks over her newly exposed skin. I reached her bare breasts and kissed each one in turn, my mouth moving slow and lingering in all the best places. Clara's back arched off the bed and she pressed into me, loving what I was doing to her. I could get used to this.

"Leo..." she half begged, half moaned. "I need... I need..."

"I know what you need, baby," I told her, breathing in the scent of her skin. "And I'm going to give it to you. Soon."

Yanking her tank top off the rest of the way, I tossed it aside. Taking hold of her wrists, I positioned both her arms above her head. I needed her still and at my mercy for what I had planned next. If this was her first time, then I would make it special. I wanted her to compare every other moment with any other man to her moments with me. Although, hopefully, there would never be a chance for her to compare. Hopefully, I was about to set the bar so high—she'd only ever need me between her legs.

Rocking back on my knees, I went for her panties. Slowly, I slipped them down her legs, leaving her completely exposed. Now that I had her very naked and practically squirming underneath me, I paused to study her for another moment. She tried to move her hands to cover her body, but I caught her wrists and placed them back above her head. "You're so damn beautiful. I always knew you would be. Let me just look for another moment," I whispered.

She let me look, her cheeks flushing under my stare. I meant to keep dragging my eyes over her body, but couldn't pull my gaze away from her face.

Heat seared across my flesh. Leaning closer to her, I kissed her cheek and whispered against her ear. "You're blushing. Are you sure you want to do this? We can go play Monopoly or watch a movie or argue about something stupid. Whatever you want. I'll be just as happy."

"Do I look like I want to play Monopoly right now?" she groaned.

I smiled. "No, you don't."

"This is what I want," she assured me, her voice breathy. "I don't think I've ever wanted anything more."

“Good. I needed to hear you say that. Are you on birth control?”

Her face turned an even darker shade of red. I hadn’t meant to embarrass her, but I didn’t have a condom so I needed to know. “Yes. Dad made us both go on it when he found Maggie and Robby in bed together that one time.”

“Thank you, Robby,” I muttered, placing both of my palms on her bare, beautiful stomach. With my knees, I nudged her legs apart. Clara laying on my bed, opened up like this for me, was nearly my undoing. I swear, I almost came right then and there. But I somehow managed to contain myself. It was my turn now to show her exactly how good sex could be.

I grabbed my length in my hand, positioning myself so close to where she was ready and waiting. Only a jerk forward…and I could be inside her. But I didn’t move inside her.

Not yet, at least.

“I don't want to wear a condom with you,” I explained. “I don't want anything between us. I promise I'm okay. It's been well over two years since I last had sex, and I've been checked since then.”

“Leo,” she grunted. Her hands still above her head, her body wiggling under my stare, her nipples perfect and hard. “Just stop teasing me.”

“Teasing?” I smiled. “I can show you teasing.”

My eyes latched onto hers and my hips moved carefully forward, the tip of my erection hitting her heat. Gasping in surprise, she bucked at our light contact. But still I didn't move inside her. Instead, keeping a firm hold of myself, I moved myself up and down, back and forth, slipping against her and spreading her wetness all over. Then I moved the head of my erection a little higher and brought it over her sweet spot. I paused for a second before moving in slow, small circles.

Oh, yes! She felt so warm, so perfect, and so damn sweet. My body started to quiver. I wasn't even really doing anything and this was already too much.

Clara's arms moved to down and she gripped firmly on my biceps. Her eyes even drifted closed. Damn. Could I get her off like this? Maybe, but I wasn't done teasing her mercifully. As soon as I was sure she was nearly ready to combust under me, I moved away.

Her eyes snapped open.

I couldn't contain my smile. "Keep still," I warned, brushing my fingers up and down her body. My hands lingered and caressed until one came to the junction of her thighs. "I'm going to kiss you now…" I warned, running a finger slowly over the center of her heat. "Here." Then I moved down to position my head between her legs, pressing my lips against her.

I know I'd shocked her because she gasped and tried to squeeze her legs together. Almost as quickly, she relaxed under me, giving into my tongue and my touch. Shit. It even surprised me how much I enjoyed this. Because she tasted sweeter than a girl ought to. My eyes flickered up to meet hers. And the look we shared was pure, fearless lust.

She shivered and I noticed as goose bumps spread across her stomach.

"Leo. Stop!" she cried.

I stopped immediately, unsure what I'd just done wrong.

Apparently nothing. Because she grabbed at my arms and yanked me up her body. "I only want to come while you're inside me," she moaned, sounding almost desperate, kissing me hard, pulling on my hips, yanking me closer to her.

Okay. I was fine with that.

Positioning myself between her legs, I began to penetrate her slowly but paused to whisper, "Don't move, baby."

Our eyes met. She didn't move.

"This part may hurt," I explained. I'd never been with a virgin, at least not to my knowledge, and I wanted to make this as painless as possible for her. “I'll do it quick. When I get inside you, I won't move for a minute so you can get used to me. Okay, killer? Then we'll take it from there. I don't want to hurt you. And if you need to stop, tell me and we will.”

Biting her lip, she didn’t deny my suspicions. “Okay, Leo. I trust you,” she said.

“Good.”

I blew out a breath I hadn’t realized I’d been holding in, while my hands gripped under her thighs. I had a serious thing for her thighs. They were soft yet strong, sexy as fuck, and I loved getting to touch her so much. I angled her hips the way I needed them. Not wasting another second, because every second I wasn’t inside her was becoming pure torture, I pressed in.

I felt it too. The moment I ripped through her virginity. I never knew it was something I could feel so easily, but I did. Like I’d promised, I stopped once inside her, hovering above her on locked arms. It was some kind of wonderful torture.

Barely a second passed before she said, “I'm used to you now. You can move.”

I smiled at her. She looked so damn pretty under me.

“Seriously, Leo. Please—start moving.” She grabbed hold of my ass, urging me to move.

And then it happened. I moved—giving into her fully. I pulled back and then wasn’t nearly as gentle as I ought to have been as I pumped inside her again. And again. She yelped these sexy moans as I continued my assault. Then her moans changed to perfect little screams. Each sound told me exactly how much she was enjoying every inch of my cock buried deep inside her. And I loved seeing this reaction coming from her. Fuck that bland, indifferent version of Clara she liked to show off to the world. Now

I knew how to bring out a very different version of the girl.

"Yes, Leo!" she cried. "God, yes!"

Her legs locked tighter around my waist, and for someone who'd never done this before, it didn't show. And I learned something new about myself…sober sex was the best kind.

As I realized this, I slowed my pace and began to control my movements. We'd been going at it fast and furious, but I needed time to slow. I needed this moment to last for as long as I could make it last. There was no finish line with Clara. And fucking her senseless, as much as my body wanted that kind of wild abandonment, wasn't how I wanted to remember our first time. My movements became soft and careful...sweet, even. I pumped slowly in and out, resting my forehead against her forehead, staring into her eyes.

We moved like this until she whispered, "Leo, please. Please."

I could tell she was close. I was closer.

Reaching my hand between us, touching her in the exact way she needed, I helped her reach her climax. Her mouth opened as if she was about to really scream but no sound came out. Watching her come was like getting to touch the sun. There would never again be anything more magnificent than this moment. The muscles deep inside her contracted against me, clutching me hard. My fingers ran across her bare breasts as she arched into me. And even when my own orgasm ripped through me, surprising me by the way it suddenly overcame my whole body, we never broke eye contact.

When my breath returned and the world started making sense again, I whispered, "Thank the fucking Lord you hit me with that golf cart."

She laughed and I didn't even attempt to hide the smile that came to my lips.

"Anytime," she joked. "And I guess I got your pants off after all."

I laughed—both happy and content with my mind at ease for, possibly, the first time ever. But when I laughed, my body moved slightly and I realized I was still hard, still buried deep inside her. We both felt this movement and both stopped laughing immediately. Electricity blasted through me.

I had to have her. Again. Now.

I pushed up onto my arms, rocking my hips gloriously in the process, and I studied Clara under me. Would she be okay if we tried this again so soon?

"Are you okay?" I whispered.

"Never better," she answered.

Ever so slowly, I eased in and out of her. "My offer to play Monopoly still stands."

"Shut the hell up, Leo. Don't be an ass."

"I'm beginning to think every time you call me an ass—or some variation of the word—it's really just a term of endearment. Am I right?"

Cupping the sides of my face, she kissed me and pressed her tongue deep into my mouth. Her kiss said everything I needed to know. I was right. Her legs wrapped around my waist and suddenly we were having sex again—the conversation, over.

From start to end, my movements stayed rhythmic, gentle, and extremely controlled. I focused on kissing and touching her as I moved, and it was pure heaven. I focused on showing her just how much I loved and cared for her. It didn't take long before she was falling apart under me all over again.

I found my release soon after she did and then we lay there, unmoving—a tangle of limbs and sweat—until our breathing returned to normal. Easing myself out of her, I was utterly spent and grabbed the corner of my duvet cover. I yanked the comforter on top of us, snuggling in closer to her warm body. A moment later I felt her drift to sleep in my arms.

I reached over, careful not to wake her, and set the alarm on my clock for morning. Clara had her golf lessons—I didn't want her to be late because of me. As I shifted back in close to her, a sleepy Clara hooked her leg around my waist, snuggling tighter against me. She was clingy while she slept. I liked it. After a little while of resting in her firm grip, I fell asleep too.

* * *

My alarm woke us before the sun. At the noise, Clara jolted in my arms. She attempted to dive for my alarm. I'm not sure what she was doing, but her legs tangled with my sheets and she fell straight to the floor. All the covers on my bed went with her.

She popped to her feet, clutching the sheet against her naked chest.

This strangely giddy, foreign noise came out of my mouth. God, I'd never woken so content and so happy in all my life. Clara was adorable. Her back-to-blonde hair hung in a wild, wavy, sexy mess around her face and she glared at me like her fall was entirely my fault.

"Not funny," she said, pressing the button to silence my alarm clock.

"Kind of funny," I countered, my voice husky from sleep. "Now, get back in bed. Please."

Blush came to her cheeks as she crawled back into bed beside me. I could tell she was nervous. Hell, she'd given up her virginity to me last night. Maybe she had a lot of emotional thoughts running through her pretty head. But I wasn't going anywhere and wasn't about to be anything but kind to her about it all, so she need not worry.

I tugged at her waist, pulling her body against my side. Then I pressed a kiss to her temple. "I was buried in you twice last night and today I plan on exceeding that number, so don't go backwards with me," I said in a low voice, trying to put any worries she might have at ease. "And I'm sorry about the alarm, baby. I set it because I know you have your golf lessons today. Forgive me? I didn't mean to wake you up like that."

"It's fine," she whispered, no anger in her voice, "but help me out of these covers before I get claustrophobic."

This was better than Christmas. The sheet tangled around her and I tried my best to keep a straight face as I helped her free. By the time the sheets came loose, my heart was racing and my breathing rate had doubled. We were now both wonderfully naked with our limbs tangled on top of the sheets.

"Are you okay?" I asked her. "You seem different today."

"It's just...you make me shy," she admitted in a whisper into my chest. "And nervous and scared and crazy-insane. And the last couple days, there's been this weird feeling in the pit of my stomach that won't go away. Fluttering. But please don't think I'm going backwards with you. It's just that…well, it's daylight and I've never been naked like this with anyone before."

Damn. And yet she was here with me now. I hooked my finger under her chin and tilted her face up toward mine. "Trust me, the feeling's mutual. Remember that day at the pool last year when you asked if I was gay?"

She rolled her eyes. "How could I ever forget that?"

"Yeah, well neither could I. You marched over in your swimsuit and laid your fine ass down beside me. I'm not sure what you were reading, but you were biting your lip and blushing. I swear, I couldn't move or think or breathe. That's the real reason I never got up to change or swim. I had to picture my Great-Grandma Bunny the whole time just to keep from embarrassing myself. I couldn't even manage to have a normal conversation with you."

The fact that she was naked and right in front of me was too much of a temptation. I swept a finger over her bare shoulder and down the length of her, stopping to trace small circles on her thigh. "So...I'm ecstatic that you're feeling some of the same things that I've *always* felt for you."

She let out a small breath, relaxing beside me. A hint of a smile touched her lips. I kept touching her thigh but she surprised me more when she began running her fingers over my chest. Her soft touch had me hard in an instant, but it was her next words that made my heart swell and burst.

"I play up the indifference thing so people don't know what I'm really feeling," she confessed. Something I already knew, because it was obvious to me. But, just the fact that she trusted me enough to tell me, had me feeling like the luckiest guy on earth.

"I know," I told her. "But when it's just you and me, you don't have to do that anymore. To hell with the rest of the world—they don't matter."

Needing her now more than ever before, I took firm hold of her waist and rolled so she was on top of me, straddling my lap. Her hands came to rest on my chest. Her breathing changed to something rough and uneven. Her nipples were puckered and right there in front of me. The sight of her in this moment was something that would be stuck in my head until the day I died.

Dammit, I could even feel how ready she was against my stomach.

Lifting her with ease, I positioned her just right, and swallowed a scream as I brought her down on my erection. Suddenly I was inside her and it was perfect.

Clara made a little o-face and a beautiful flush crossed her skin.

"Last night, I was scared too."

Her eyes bore into mine. "You were?" she breathed, shifting and rocking ever-so-slightly against me. "Is that...um...why you froze up on me?"

"Yes. Then you dropped down to your knees and I realized I was your first. No man can ignore the gravity of those unspoken words."

She rocked against me again, and I gave her what her body and mine were both screaming for. Clutching her waist, I lifted her up and lowered her gently back down, pushing as deep as I could go inside her. "Why were you still a virgin, Clara?" I bit out. "You're the most impulsive person I know, but you never felt the need to chase after *that* impulse?"

Things had been slow, easy, and nice last night, but now I needed rough. So I held her close and flipped us both so that I could be on top. Too many emotions were running crazily through my head. Once I was on top, I began slamming in and out of her. No longer able to hold a proper conversation, I spoke between ragged breaths. "Tell. Me. Please."

"Because..." she gasped.

My movements continued as she struggled to answer. I don't know why, but everything seemed a little better this morning. Like having sex in broad daylight made it more real somehow. And I liked that. My body climbed higher and higher even though I was still waiting on her answer. "Shit, Clara. Just answer me."

"Because..." she rasped. "Because…I love you."

What.

The.

Fuck?

Of anything she could have said I never would have expected that. A moment after those wonderful words left her lips, Clara screamed out as an orgasm rocked through her. Her fingers dug into my skin as she bit down against my shoulder, while I continued to fuck her hard. The way she came undone under me was nothing short of amazing.

The moment was so unexpected and so perfect, that I couldn't help the way I followed. I felt my balls in my throat just before the first wave of pleasure raged through me too. Then another and another and another hit me, until I had nothing left to give. I stilled, my weight resting on top of her.

Wow.

Pulling out, I fell onto the bed beside her, exhausted and exhilarated all at once.

But Clara wasn't quite so content. She scrambled out of my bed and started to dress as fast as possible. She hadn't meant to tell me she loved me—that much was obvious. What I didn't understand was why it was such a big deal that she did.

Because suddenly it was.

The way she trudged around my room, collecting her clothes from yesterday, yanking everything on at hyper speed…it was very clear that she'd become incredibly uncomfortable very fast.

"I have my lessons," she mumbled as if it was some sort of an apology. She avoided my eyes like the plague. I was out of bed, watching her with my stomach in my throat. She'd calm down in a minute and realized she had nothing to fear. Right? I wasn't sure. It was always hard to tell with Clara.

She had on everything else, but couldn't seem to find her shirt. One arm covered her tits like a Band-Aid as she searched the floor. "Dad's going to kill me if I'm late again," she groaned.

I took a calming breath. "You still have thirty minutes."

"Have you seen my tank top? Or do you have some kind of shirt I can borrow? Like a white t-shirt or something?" Her voice was as ridged as her posture as she glared at me from across the room.

Shit. That wall of indifference of hers…it was back up.

My stomach turning to acid, I moved for my dresser. Opening a drawer

I found her one of my white t-shirts. Taking it in my hand, I walked across the room to give it to her. She reached out, but as she grabbed for that damn shirt, my fingers wouldn't let go.

God, now we were playing tug-o-war over a shirt.

Her eyes were fierce. "Give me the shirt, Leo."

She won. I let go in an instant, adding, "It's not going to fit you." My voice came out all gritty. I was never one to let emotions overcome me, but tears were threatening to swell in my eyes. I didn't have the first fucking clue as to what I'd done wrong. Because this couldn't be about her three little words. Whatever had set her off was more than that.

She yanked the shirt over her head and then dared a glance up at me. The look she gave me screamed *why you*? Like she was suddenly shocked to find herself in *my* bedroom of all places.

I reached up to touch her face, wanting to do something to ease all her fears. But my hand dropped away and something ferocious shot through my veins. Anger. It was a son of bitch and it hit me hard.

Clenching my jaw, trying not to say anything I would regret, I turned away from her to get dressed. I realized how naked I was standing in front of her and a small shiver of embarrassment ran through me. I didn't bother with fresh clothes and instead put on my day-old clothes I found on the floor. "This is the part where I lose my temper," I told her, my voice much more even and controlled than I felt on the inside. "We just spent a great night together—the best of my life—and now you're being ridiculous. Fucking ridiculous."

"Don't call me ridiculous," she spat back at me.

My eyes narrowed. "I call it like I see it, sweetheart. Is it really so terrifying to love me? If so, then go on—run off if that's what you have to do. But don't expect me to always chase after you when you pull this kind of bullshit."

We stared at each other for several long heartbeats. Both of us falling right back into our usual roles.

"Whatever," she shrugged, as if she didn't give a shit. And honest to God, I couldn't tell anymore if she was just protecting herself or if this unaffected hatred toward me was how she truly felt. "Bye, Leo."

Without so much as a flinch or a tear or any indication that she felt as broken as I did, she turned and left my room.

And the second I heard the front door slam, I dropped to my knees.

CHAPTER 17:

It took me about ten minutes to realize that I shouldn't have let Clara leave my house. Ten minutes I couldn't get back. Ten minutes that would probably haunt me for the rest of my life. I decided that this wasn't over between us—that it couldn't be. That I wasn't going to let it end so randomly and ridiculously. Yes, ridiculously. I hopped in my car and raced for the Pro Shop.

Clara wasn't there. And worse, according to Mary Ann, she'd called about five minutes earlier and cancelled all her golf lessons over the next two weeks.

"This is so typical of Clara," Mary Ann chirped, spinning around in her desk chair to wag her finger at me. "Maggie would never act so ungrateful. But Clara…I expected this from her."

"Well, I didn't," I told her firmly. "And you should watch what you say about *either* of Reed's daughters. It's not smart to talk shit about the boss's family. Unless you're purposely trying to lose your job."

Before she could respond, I turned and left the Pro Shop.

Now I was in a bad place. I struggled with all my addictions on a normal day—add a little turmoil to the mix and I became the person I hated most. My father had nothing on me.

And right now I craved something strong to take the edge off, something to make me forget. Having had Clara, however briefly, and then losing her…well, it was much worse than never having her at all. I knew that now. I wanted to hit or break something. My head was in a horrible place. And it was killing me inside knowing that Clara was probably hurting too—hurting because in her moment of weakness I'd been an asshole to her when that was the last thing she deserved.

Not trusting myself to be alone, I went straight to the Ryder house.

Maybe Clara would be there. I hoped like hell she would be there. But if she wasn't than I needed to be around my family while I waited for her to come home. Because these people were my family. It occurred to me now, something I'd always known but never fully accepted, that they were more my family than my own blood. And I needed to just *be* around them right now, before I did something stupid.

"Morning," I said to whoever was listening as I let myself into the Ryder house. I cut straight through the kitchen. There were people present, but my eyes didn't even register who because I couldn't function right now. "I'm going to go lie on your couch for a while. So, yeah, just ignore me."

Disappearing as quickly as I'd appeared, I headed into the living room, automatically clicking on the TV. Not one second later, Maggie entered the room, standing at the foot of the couch I'd stretched out on.

"That had to have been your most dramatic entrance ever." Her voice shook a little. "What are you doing on my couch?"

"Wallowing," I mumbled, trying to focus on the TV. My whole idea about needing to be around other people suddenly seemed like a horrible idea. I was terrible company.

"What happened?"

I tried to swallow down the giant lump that had been stuck in my throat since Clara ran away from me. It didn't go anywhere, so I gritted my teeth and talked through it. “Nothing I want to talk about,” I assured her.

“You're scaring me a little.”

“I'm peaches.”

Peaches was a code-word I used with Maggie. It meant “I’ll-pretend-I’m-fine-because-that’s-what-I’m-supposed-to-do-but-really-I’m-not-fine.” Clara had referenced this very word before she’d dumped beer on my head in the Alligator Lounge. And now that was the memory that clouded everything else. I deserved that beer dumping. I deserved all this too.

Maggie came around the couch and sat on the coffee table, blocking my view of the TV. I had no choice but to look at her. I gave her a look and she seemed to read my mind.

“Okay, fine,” she groaned. “If you don’t want to talk then I’ll talk first. There's something I need to tell you anyway. The last couple days, I thought I was in love with—”

“Jesus H. Christ,” Reed huffed, marching into the room before Maggie could confess she was probably still in love with Robby. I might have been glad for his interruption too if Reed didn’t look so terrified. He clutched his phone tightly in his hand. A woman—I can’t recall her name but she’d been working for Reed for years—came into the room behind him, her face as pale as Reed’s.

“I just got off the phone with Mary Ann at the Pro Shop,” Reed said, shaking his head. *Oh God, here it comes.* “Clara never showed up for her lessons. She did call, however, telling Mary Ann she was sorry she had to cancel *all of them*.”

Reed’s words permeated the air. “I'm trying to decide if I should be angry or worried.” His attention shifted to me. “Which is it, son?”

Shit. The distinct impression that Clara’s sudden disappearance this morning was more than temporary washed over me. She had issues with Maggie, issues with Reed, and issues with me. Maybe the way I forced her into admitting her feelings during sex was only a fraction of what sent her running.

I sat up, running one shaky hand through my hair, while the tension in the room grew so thick I could barely breathe. “Worried,” I muttered. Then I stood and walked away as fast as I could manage without running.

Fuck staying sober.

Halfway down her driveway, nearly to my car, I heard Maggie yelling after me. “Leo! Wait!”

I didn’t wait. “Not now, Mags!” I snapped, yanking open my car door.

“Yes, now!” she screamed, wrapping both of her small hands around one of my arms, pulling against my strength. Wow. I never knew polite Maggie could be so fierce. “You are NOT going to run off to get drunk or high or whatever it is you do when you *think* you can't handle your problems! I won't let you this time! I just won't!”

“I'm fine.”

“No, you aren't! Don't think I never notice all of your attempts to self-medicate because I do—constantly! And do any of them ever work for you? No! So, please...don't go.”

Taking a deep breath, I stopped fighting her and closed my car door.

Someone else had noticed my *habits*. Clara had noticed and it seemed Maggie had too. That killed me. I hadn’t meant to drag other people into my problems.

I let out a sigh and wrapped my arms around Maggie. How many times had she used me as a shoulder to cry on when all her relationships went up in flames? And now our roles were suddenly reversed.

Several minutes passed before we broke apart. She glanced up at me tentatively.

“What happened?” she whispered.

I guess I needed to tell her everything now. “When we were in New

York, Clara asked me to prove to her I wasn't an ass. She wanted to let me in and I think maybe she did. And the first chance she gave me to prove myself, I ruined everything—story of my fucking life. Why is it that I can't control my temper around her?"

Mags gave me a small smile. "Because you love her. We all do stupid things when we're in love."

"Then I must be the biggest moron there ever was."

She suddenly burst out laughing. "You and me both. Dean shows back up, confusing the heck out of me, and the last couple days I somehow convinced myself I was in love with *you!* Omigosh!"

"Me?" I demanded. "What?"

"Yes, you." Still laughing, she rested her hands on her knees as if to catch her breath. "I was even going to kiss you to try to figure out who I liked more, you or him. If that's not moronic, then I don't know what is." Her laughter died as she finished her sentence.

Um? Okay. Wasn't expecting that. And now I was seriously confused and dazed, bewildered and shocked.

"So, you don't love me then?" I asked, terrified out of my ever-loving mind.

"No. Sorry, not like that."

I let out a huge sigh of relief. "Thank the fucking Lord."

She smacked me. "Hey, you don't have to be mean about it."

The corners of my mouth twitched upward ever so slightly. I'm not sure what had been going on with Maggie or if it was really just Robby who'd driven her to become so confused, but it made me feel a little better knowing that I wasn't the only one dealing with drama out their eyeballs. I guess most people get so caught up in their own shit that they hardly notice the shit other people are going through. I needed to pay better attention.

"So," she said to me, "this older, wiser, very sexy guy told me a couple of days ago that I had to fight for what I wanted—"

"Me?"

"No, Dean." She rolled her eyes. "You're two months younger than me, silly. Anyway, Dean told me that I shouldn't let the moment pass without fighting for what I wanted. How many times in your life did you say something nasty to Clara, instead of grabbing and kissing her or telling her how much you really cared about her? I'm guessing a lot. Same goes for me. I stuck with Andrew for four years—*four years!*—and now I can't even remember why. So, let's do this. We have to fight for the people we love or else you're going to end up like your father—a cold bastard who has more money than God but nothing to really show for it—and I'll end up a trophy wife in a loveless marriage with someone like Andrew."

I smiled. This was the first time I'd ever heard her swear. And she had a very good point. The last person I wanted to be was my father. "Did you just say *bastard,* Maggie?"

"Shut up!" She walked around to the other side of my car. "C'mon. Let's go find Clara. We both have some groveling to do. I haven't been exactly nice to her over the years either."

We climbed in the car. I felt instantly better.

* * *

Better didn't last long. Who knew Clara was some kind of Houdini? I swear to God this wasn't out of the blue because the girl disappeared without a trace. Twenty-four hours had passed and I hadn't eaten, slept, showered, or spoken much. I wasn't even craving alcohol anymore. I'd just turned kind of numb. This wasn't even about me and my heartbreak anymore—it was about Clara and the fact that we were all seriously worried about her.

Reed had called the credit card company and Clara had to be using cash because her credit card hadn't been used in a few days. No one—seriously, no one, and Maggie had asked everyone—had seen her since she went missing.

I tried calling her and messaging her on Facebook. Then, at my lowest and my most desperate point, I wrote her the sappiest email ever and sent that. No response. Everything proved to be useless. Clara had disappeared into thin air and part of me, though I wouldn't voice it out loud, feared it might be for good.

After another twenty-four hours passed and I wanted to call the police.

Reed talked me out of it.

"Give it another couple days," he assured me. "Clara's her mother's daughter. Maggie…well, she's always been more like me. And Clara has Carol's personality"

It was shocking to hear Reed talking about his dead wife. She was never brought up. Never. Even more shocking was when he mentioned my mom next.

"One time," Reed continued. "Right before our wedding, Carol and your mother stole my car and drove to Mexico. I was left with the last minute wedding plans and left wondering if she'd even show up at the church. Hell, she was three months pregnant with twins and I was scared out of my mind that I might never see her again. But I did. Carol was there—in her wedding gown, beautiful as ever, walking down that aisle in front of all our friends, like she'd never gone missing in the first place. She smiled at me, told me she loved me, and everything was okay. She told me later that evening that she'd just needed a few days alone to think and make sure she was making her decision out of love rather than obligation since she was pregnant. That was Carol's style. When things got rough—often she just needed to back off, cool down, and reemerge stronger than ever. And with time, rather than running off to Mexico, I became the person she backed off with. Her safe place, so to speak."

My jaw tight and my eyes stinging, I nodded. I understood what he was saying. "Thanks, Reed," I whispered. I knew what I needed to do now.

CHAPTER 18:

Another twenty-four hours later and Maggie and I were sitting on a plane, halfway to New York City. After two days of *wallowing*, something in me had snapped this morning. Suddenly I felt confident and excited all over again. What Reed had told me about Clara's mom resonated deep inside me. I'd started to believe that Clara would come home, but more importantly I had shit to do to prepare for that moment. Some things needed to happen first.

"I have an errand to run and then we're going to Brooklyn."

"That's fine," Maggie answered.

We'd been forced to fly commercial since my dad currently had the family jet. Worse yet, we were stuck in coach. Sure, I was a trust fund baby with a couple million in the bank—yes, millions but not billions. But since I wasn't exactly sure what the future held for me in this moment, if I would end up pissing off my dad when I didn't return to work in the week he'd given me, I decided that spending thousands of dollars on a last minute first-class plane ticket wasn't practical. I'd never been the least bit conservative with my money, but today that changed.

So for the first time in my life, I was on an airplane sitting in coach. It was cramped, there was a screaming toddler in the row behind Maggie and me, nobody told me food wouldn't be served so my stomach was growling, but overall it wasn’t too bad. Okay, I lied. It sucked.

But I’d do whatever for Clara.

The plane reached JFK and we hurried through the airport. We hadn't brought bags and our return tickets were booked for a flight home in six hours. We were pressing our time and our luck.

Outside the airport, I claimed a yellow taxi from the long line that waited by the curb. I preferred having my own driver, but there wasn’t any time for that and I didn’t want my dad knowing I was in the city. The second the taxi door slammed shut, I pulled a few hundreds out and handed them over to the driver.

“I'm going to need your services for the whole day. Well, roughly five or six hours.”

The driver stared wide-eyed at the wad of cash in my hands.

“Is that gonna be cool?” I demanded.

The man nodded. “Whatever, man.”

“Good. Now head to Harry Winston. Fifth Avenue. And, please, drive as fast as you can.”

“Are you kidding me?” Maggie shouted, choking and gasping for a decent breath of air. “Harry Winston! As in the jeweler, HARRY WINSTON?”

Dramatic much?

“Relax and buckle your seat belt,” I deadpanned.

The taxi driver zipped the car into traffic, causing Maggie’s body to lurch into the door. Her eyes widened and she hurried to buckle her seat belt. Then she returned to scolding me. “You're nuts! You can't be serious about this.”

There was only one reason a guy would go to Harry Winston…but a wedding ring wasn’t my intention at all. Hell, if I wanted Clara to run screaming in the opposite direction—kind of like she’d already done—then a wedding ring would be my best bet. And, yes, I had every intention of marrying Clara *one day*, if the stars aligned and she'd let me. But not yet. Right now I had something else in mind. And I may have skimped on the plane tickets today, but I wouldn't skimp on this.

"I know what I'm doing," I said, trying to assure her.

Maggie grew quiet after that, but I could tell she was dying to say more. We reached the Upper East Side and Fifth Avenue in record time. Regina stood at the curb, waiting for us just like I'd asked of her earlier. "I won't be long," I told Maggie and the driver. "I'm dropping something off and then we can head to Brooklyn."

"No." Before I could jump out of the cab, Maggie suddenly grabbed hold of my arm. "I don't trust Regina."

"What? You've never mentioned this before."

"I know. She's probably a great assistant and I have no clue what you need *her* to do for you at Harry Winston, but I don't trust her."

"Okay then," I simply said, shrugging. I trusted Maggie so if she didn't trust Regina then I couldn't let her anywhere near this project of mine. It was too important to gamble on. I stepped out of the car.

"Hi, Mr. Maddox." Regina smiled. "May I ask why I'm standing in front of Harry Winston?"

"I'm sorry, Regina. I'm sorry you came all the way over here, but I don't need your assistance after all. You can head back to the hotel."

She turned in a huff and hurried away. I'd never seen her do anything that wasn't completely proper and lady-like. Maybe there was something behind Maggie's suspicions. Who knows? I didn't have time to dwell on it though. I had an appointment with a jeweler.

* * *

A half hour later, I came out of the store empty-handed.

"Did you get what you needed?" Maggie demanded as I returned to the car.

I sat back in my seat, relaxing a little. "Yes."

"Can I see?"

"It's not ready, but I called Great-Grandma Bunny, since you don't trust Regina. She said she'd be able to pick everything up and meet us back at the airport."

Maggie laughed. "She's ninety!"

"She's fine." My great-grandma loved me more than anyone else on earth. And I knew this because she was mean as hell to everyone but me. She would do anything for me. And, even at ninety, she was lucid as I was.

I leaned forward and told the driver, "The Alligator Lounge in Brooklyn."

Time to go find Stephany.

Maggie shot me a look like I'd just told the driver to take me to a strip club, but she didn't say anything as the cab made its way across town.

"Let me do the talking," I insisted when we stepped out of the cab and paused outside the bar. I glanced upward to the canvas sign hanging above us. It's funny how different things look the second time around—always less glamorous somehow. Or maybe daylight always has that kind of an effect on bars. "You stand there and look pretty," I told Maggie, turning my attention back to her and raising my eyebrows.

"Hey now," she barked, pretending to be offended.

"You know what I mean. And if it comes to it...do your thing."

She nodded, knowing exactly what I meant.

When I was in the right mood, and I could control my anger, it was easy for me to manipulate people with my words. And when she felt like it, it was easy for Maggie to manipulate using her looks.

We ventured inside. The place was slow since it was a Thursday afternoon. And as my eyes settled on the bar, I noticed my favorite bartender working today. Yippee. This was going to be fun. So fun. I approached the same guy I'd argued with over Clara's seat the first time I stepped foot into this place.

"I'm looking for Stephany Mallory," I said to him. No use beating around the bush.

"Not here," he answered. God, he was an even bigger douche than I remembered.

"And when is she working again?" I asked, a little anger seeping into my voice. "Tonight? Tomorrow? Steph's friend is missing—the girl with the purple hair, the one you met the other night—and we could really use your help."

The bartender shot Maggie a confused look. "Look, man," he said, his eyes shifting nervously back to mine. "I think you should leave. I can't give out personal information like that. Is there some sort of *special* place I can call for you?"

"What?" I asked, growing enraged. He said 'special' like he meant mental hospital.

I wanted to throw him in a mental hospital.

Maggie giggled—all giddy and light. And I knew it was *game on*. No more wasting time. She could see that I wasn't going to get anywhere with this douche…and so she took over.

"Leo means my twin," Maggie said, acting innocent. She fingered a strand of her hair, tilting her head like a life-sized doll, giving him a giant smile. "There are two of us, silly. And I would never dye my hair purple."

"Oh," the bartender answered, smiling back at her. "Gotcha." Then he winked. Ew.

I huffed, giving Maggie a staged glare and then turning my evil stare at the guy. "Can you fucking help us or not?" I grunted.

"Not," the guy said flatly.

I turned and left the bar in a huff.

Maggie could be a vampire—because she could compel the shit out of people. Maybe the girl would get all tongue-tied around her sister, but around an unsuspecting boy—she could turn lethal. Witnessing it in action kind of freaked me out and I got pissy on purpose with the bartender just so I had an excuse to wait outside. I couldn't watch her be so fake.

Her niceness, enhanced by her pretty face, was why everyone liked her so easily. But just like I played up my arrogance and Clara played up her indifference—Maggie played up her sweet and innocent act.

I guess we all had something to hide. Frankly, though, I was kind of over all these bullshit facades we were putting on.

Roughly five minutes passed—me pacing the sidewalk, scratching the scar on the inside of my wrist like it was a mosquito bite, waiting on Maggie. Finally the door to the bar opened and she walked out.

"Please tell me that worked, Mags."

Then I noticed Stephany follow her outside. Holy shit. It worked. Way better than I expected, too.

"Thank God," I told Stephany. "Were you inside the whole time?"

Stephany's cheeks went pink. "Yes, sorry."

"She was hiding," Maggie blurted out.

I frowned. "Why?"

"Because I know where Clara is." Stephany shifted from one foot to another, avoiding eye contact with me. "I might not agree with everything Clara does," she continued, "but I'm not gonna tell you where she is either. I would never betray her trust like that...even if it was for her own good."

"Okay then." I shrugged. On the inside I was screaming, but on the outside I remained calm. Stephany was our first and only link to Clara. I couldn't do or say anything stupid right now that could harm that link.

"You don't have to tell us anything. But Maggie and I did come all this way, so could you at least let her know we were here, that her whole family is worried, and that we *all* want her to come home? Not just me...well, maybe especially me...but could you please tell her that?"

Stephany nodded, her head bowed and her eyes on the cement below. "I'm sorry I can't help more."

"We'll figure out another way to find her," I said, giving Stephany a quick hug. "But Maggie and I have to go now or we'll miss our plane home." Taking Maggie's arm, I pulled her quickly away from the girl and toward our waiting taxi. It took all my composure and willpower to not try to drag more information out of Stephany.

"What are you doing?" Maggie whispered. "We still have two hours before the flight."

Ignoring her question, I instead counted slowly under my breath. *Stephany would crack and help us,* I assured myself. She just had to. *One one-thousand, two one-thousand...* Then, just as we reached the taxi and I reached five one-thousand, I heard footsteps racing down the sidewalk.

"Wait," Stephany cried. "I'm coming with."

"And they don't call me Leo Maddox for nothing," I mumbled to Maggie.

The plane ride home was dreadfully boring. Great-Grandma Bunny had met me at the airport, as promised, and she'd handed over my package from Harry Winston. She'd sweetly given me a kiss on the cheek then pinched Maggie's ass and told her she'd put on some weight. Oh God, she was a handful, but I said nothing because I was beyond grateful she'd come to my aid today.

That had been a few hours ago and now we were in my car, driving the familiar route home to Blue Creek. The sun sank low on the horizon and I had Stephany, my link to Clara, in the car with us. Uncomfortable silence had been lingering all day.

As we were nearly home, Maggie was the first to speak. "Is it going to be okay that you're missing work?" she asked Stephany.

"I'll call in sick tomorrow at my internship," Stephany replied, her eyes glued to the window. "They're pretty laid back there, so I'm hoping it won't be a big deal. And I explained everything to Jesse, the bartender you were shamelessly flirting with in order to solicit information, and he agreed to cover my Saturday shift."

Maggie's eyes met mine in the rearview mirror. I wasn't sure if she was trying to pull out information from the girl or just making polite conversation.

"Sorry if that made you uncomfortable," Maggie told her. "He was cute, but I'd never date anyone with all those tattoos. Not my thing."

I almost laughed. Maggie didn't know that I had a growing obsession with marking my own body. Not that I'd care if she approved or not, but I doubted she would have made that comment had she known what lay beneath my shirt.

"When we get home," Maggie suddenly said to me, "I need you to go somewhere with me as soon as we drop off Stephany at the house. I came with you on your crazy trip to New York and now I need you to do the same for me."

"Okay," I said without hesitation. Even though I knew her crazy plan had something to do with Robby, I agreed because that was what friends did. "I can do that."

When we reached Blue Creek, we dropped Stephany off at the Ryder house. Apparently she'd been there several times before and already knew Reed, so it wouldn't be too awkward for her to be alone with him. Then Maggie gave me directions and I drove her over to one very rundown apartment complex—Robby's very rundown apartment complex.

CHAPTER 19:

Torture me while I'm at my lowest. That was what it felt like walking up to Robby's apartment. This was about the last thing I needed or wanted to do. But when I saw the outside of the building a new emotion hit me—guilt. Because this place was shady as hell and not for kids. I didn't want to feel anything for Robby, but I did. Especially knowing I had a giant unused house sitting across town and this place was all he had.

"This is it?" I asked, still stuck staring at the dilapidated building. "Please tell me he does not live here."

Maggie flinched. "It's not that bad. Well...the inside's kind of nice."

"Fine." I cut the ignition to my car. "Go tell the bastard you're in love with him. Then you both can ride off into the sunset on white horses or some shit like that."

"You think this is a mistake?" she asked, sensing my sarcasm.

I shrugged. "Honestly, I don't know if we can trust him or not. Six years ago I would have said 'go for it' without hesitation. But now... I'm usually good at seeing through people's shit, but I can't tell with him and that pisses me off."

"Then that's why you're coming inside with me."

Groaning, I gave Maggie a look.

"Remember New York? Now move it!" Maggie barked, playfully.

Half-laughing, half-groaning, I exited the car. I still wasn't sure about Robby. But truth be told, good or bad, this wasn't something I wanted to miss. Maggie followed me out of the car and clutched my arm with very shaky hands as we walked up the steps that lead into an open breezeway.

Damn, the girl was a mess. She could barely walk—that was how nervous she was. Robby better have only nice things to say to my friend or I was going to chew his ass out.

"I've never seen you like this," I told her as we reached the door. The first smile in days spread to my lips as I knocked on the door. "This is gonna be entertaining."

Robby answered a second later—dripping wet, wearing only a towel. Yeah. Ew. The towel was pink and obviously his daughter's. I could almost see Robby Jr, and it seriously grossed me out. But his image had the opposite effect on Maggie. She just stood there, stunned and not speaking.

"What are you two doing here?" Robby asked. The annoyance in his voice was clear. His eyes shifted from Maggie to me and then back to Maggie. "This isn't something I need to see...and it's late."

Poor Maggie. Her gaze wouldn't budge from his naked chest. "Um? We...um."

"Close your mouth, Mags," I muttered, "before you start drooling."

She swallowed hard.

"You can't keep showing up at my place," Robby grunted. "Especially with Leo. It's messing with my head."

What? Did he think Maggie and I were together?

"I'm messing with *your* head?" There was Maggie's voice. She found it and it came out harsh. "What about you messing with *my* head? Acting like you care one minute and then telling me *you can't* the next. That's pretty much the very definition of messing with a person's head!"

I huffed. "He thinks you and I are together because we showed up here together. That's what he means by 'messing with his head,' Mags. Calm down."

"So you're not together?" The anger mellowed in Robby immediately, and was replaced with what sounded like hope.

"No," I answered.

"Why are you here then?" he asked.

"Why do you think she's here? To wash your damn dishes?" God, some people were so dumb sometimes. I groaned and shoved past Robby, moving into his apartment. Now that he knew I wasn't there 'with' Maggie, the guy looked like he was ready to jump her bones. They seemed to need a moment alone and so I gave it to them. "I'll be on the couch. Where's the rugrat?"

"She's already in bed," Robby whispered, not paying me anymore attention as I disappeared into his apartment.

No longer able to hear their declarations of love or whatever the hell was happening at Robby's front door, I took in my surroundings. Um, yeah. The inside wasn't better than the outside. The furniture looked as if it came with the shitty apartment. And what few belongings Robby had weren't much. I sat on the couch, leaning against a pink heart pillow.

Well…at least the pink heart pillow smelled clean.

Closing my eyes, my mind drifted to Clara. *Where the hell in the world was she right now?* Did she even think of me? Did she miss me? Because that was the worst part of her running away. I missed her terribly. I missed her sassy attitude, her gentle kisses, the way she snuggled close to me when she slept, her smell, her hair—everything.

My eyes snapped open at the sound of Maggie and Robby coming into the living room.

"Did you guys kiss and make up?" I asked, rubbing at my eyes. Damn, I was tired.

Maggie sat down in a chair across the room from me. "Yes," she answered.

Okay then.

"Good," I answered, genuinely meaning it. If she was willing to forgive Robby then I suppose I was, too. "I'm gonna get going then. Call me in the morning. I need to come up with a new plan for finding Clara. I think Stephany's going to be a dead end. She's clearly worried about her—I don't think she would have come home with us if she wasn't—but she's not going to crack."

"What's going on with Clara?" Robby asked, seeming legitimately worried.

"She ran away," Maggie answered with a shrug. "Leo got in an argument with her and then she disappeared a couple days ago. We're all pretty worried this time."

"I was an ass," I told the room, "and she won't even answer her phone. We already checked her friend's place in New York and she wasn't there, so I don't know where she could be."

Robby scratched at his jawline. "She probably went to Arizona then."

What. The. Fuck.

"Arizona?" I asked, my heart falling to my shoes. That felt like half a world away.

"Yeah," Robby answered. "She mentioned it once or twice to me way back when. I can't really remember, but I think she used to call it her 'Arizona Escape Plan.'"

Maggie and I both just stared at him for several long moments. But the weirdest part was, Arizona seemed to click in my mind somehow as well. Maybe she'd mentioned this 'Escape Plan' before—years ago—when she'd been upset about something stupid. Had her juvenile threats to run away been real? Why Arizona? And could she even pull off something like that?

She'd need money. But knowing Clara, I wouldn't doubt that she had some stashed away for this very purpose.

"Thank you, Dean," I mumbled, meaning it.

And I can't believe I actually called him Dean. Yeah, *that* wasn't happening again.

He sighed. "I'm not sure I did anything. Arizona is a big state."

"It's more than I knew two minutes ago," I said sincerely. "Now...could you please go put some clothes on, pack a bag, and grab the rugrat? I'm sick of looking at you in that towel and this neighborhood isn't safe enough for a kid. I'm actually a little afraid that my car's been stolen in the fifteen minutes we've been inside your place. I have a giant home with enough rooms to house an army, and you and the kid can come stay with me until you figure out something better. Or stay however long you want. Whatever. Just go put on a damn shirt already."

A cheesy grin lit up Robby's face and then he walked over to me. And he hugged me. The bastard actually hugged me. I was so caught off-guard that for several seconds I stood still, letting this awkward moment happen.

Then I realized he was touching me and immediately pushed Robby away. "Don't turn this into a bromance. Go put on some fucking clothes."

Robby laughed before turning and heading through a doorway. Maggie mouthed a quick *omigosh* in my direction and then quietly followed after him.

Um, once again, awkward.

I waited in the living room, while those two did God knows what behind that closed door. A few moments later they reemerged, Robby dressed and holding a packed bag, while Maggie's cheeks were bright red.

I didn't even want to know.

Robby went and collected his daughter from her bedroom. She turned out to be incredibly cute and polite—with his dark hair and eyes. Then our little group headed back across town. This was going to be interesting. Part of me was surprised Robby had agreed to come stay with me so easily. Part of me dreaded it. And a third part of me was strangely relieved.

We dropped Maggie at her house because it was late and Stephany probably would appreciate the company. Then Robby, the kid—Valerie, her name was Valerie—and I went back to my place.

Valerie had the widest eyes as we stepped through the front door. "Sorry about the mess," I said, pointing off at the cluttered den. "I'm redecorating, possibly renovating, but will probably need to hire someone because I don't have a clue what I'm doing."

"Hmm," Robby said, glancing around. "You know, that's what I do. Renovations. Mostly bars. Maybe, in exchange for staying here, I could help you. Or not. It's whatever you're comfortable with."

Standing there, with Valerie's bag in my hand, I nodded. "Yeah, whatever," I answered. But to be honest, all this nice-guy crap was starting to make me feel itchy. I needed Clara. I was on edge and until I knew she was safe, nothing was going to calm me down. "Let me just show you which rooms you can take."

Marching up the long staircase, my phone started to buzz in my pocket. Anytime I received a phone call over the past few days, it kept causing my heart to flip in my chest. And it thudded extra hard this time. Wanting it to be Clara so desperately, I pulled out my phone to check the screen.

Random number. Virginia area code. Possibly a Blue Creek number. Not Clara.

I sighed, answering. "Hello."

No answer, but someone was there on the other line, breathing a little too heavy.

"Hello?" I asked again, groaning. "I can hear you breathing on the other line. If you're selling something, I already own it and—"

“Who is it?” Robby asked me. He’d just helped Valerie get comfortable in Great-Grandma Bunny’s bedroom. The room was drowning in flowers, gaudy and hideous—so why did everyone always choose her old room to stay in?

“I don't know,” I told him. A strange feeling overtook me. The person on the other line hadn’t spoken a word, but they hadn’t hung up either. Holy shit. Maybe it was Clara.

“Look,” I mumbled quickly to Robby. “There's plenty of food in the kitchen, towels in all the bathrooms...help yourself, okay?”

He nodded and immediately I disappeared down the hall, into my room.

“Clara?” I whispered softly, my heart racing and a lump clogging up my throat as I leaned against my bedroom door. It had to be her. “I know it's you and don't you dare hang up on me.”

No response. Okay, I could deal with that.

“Your mysterious silence tells me it's you, baby,” I uttered, kind of loving that she’d called me this way. As if she’d needed to hear my voice and couldn’t resist or something. “You don't have to say anything. I realized something today. That—”

The other line clicked, dead. *Had she hung up on me?* My panicked fingers hurried to redial the number she’d called from. But when I tried calling her back, it went straight to voicemail. Like the phone she’d called me from had died.

I had to believe Clara hadn’t hung up on me.

Breathing heavily, I stared at the number for several long seconds. For shits and giggles, I texted it to my detective friend. About five minutes later he text me back. The guy sure was reliable. Turns out the number belonged to someone else I knew.

Leah Longerburger.

I wasn't very fond of Leah—not now and certainly not in the past when I was losing my virginity to her in a desperate act to lose it to anything that moved and looked pretty—but I did what I had to do and headed straight for her house.

CHAPTER 20:

From there everything else fell into place. All I had to do was show up at Leah's moderately-sized house and immediately she started offering up information like I was holding her down and torturing it out of her. She handed me Clara's phone and confessed that Clara had run away to Phoenix. They exchanged phones and Leah had even given her a credit card to borrow. Then she begged me not to tell Clara about *our* past.

"What?" I asked, stunned. That was the furthest thing from my mind right this moment. The few times we'd hooked up happened years ago. And I'd been so wasted, I wasn't sure if I could accurately remembered the experience.

"Clara's like my *only* real friend," Leah pleaded, running her fingers frantically through hair. "She's nice to me when most people treat me like shit. Please don't tell her we used to screw. Seriously, please. I'll do anything."

"Yeah, seriously, I'll tell her whatever the hell I want."

"Shit, Leo. Do you always have to be such an asshole?"

I smiled. "Yes, I do." Then I started to walk away.

"Maybe if you weren't such a dick then I would have told you which hotel she's staying at," she shouted after me.

I stopped, turning around briefly. "I love Clara. I've always loved

Clara. Even when I was screwing you I loved her. So yeah, if she wants to know about my past then I'll be honest with her. Okay? I don't care if that hurts your friendship with her or not."

Then I left, not bothering to ask which hotel Clara was staying at. I already knew. My gut was screaming the truth at me. Mine. She'd chosen a Maddox to stay at. And I knew this simply because I knew Clara. She'd want at least a little something familiar.

By the time I got home, Maggie was waiting for me. Turns out she'd done a search of Clara's room and found lots of computer printouts on Phoenix. That was it—knowing she'd thought about this whole 'Arizona Escape Plan' long before me and knowing her little ass was probably snuggled tight in one of *my* hotel beds right now—I had to go to her. I couldn't wait any longer.

* * *

So here we were at the airport—Maggie, Robby, Valerie, Stephany, Reed, Anita, and I. The whole fam-damn-ily. Anita was the woman who had been at Reed's the other morning during my *wallowing*. Why the hell she'd tagged along was beyond me? Maybe she and Reed were dating. It didn't matter. All that mattered was that we were going to Arizona. We were getting Clara back.

Slipping into the nearest bathroom, I needed a moment alone before we boarded our flight. I'd never been so terrified in my entire life. I could boast about my confidence and inflated ego all day long, but when it came to the possibilities surrounding my future with Clara, I suddenly turned into that scared little boy hiding in his father's library. I wanted her and I didn't know what I would do if it turned out she didn't want me back.

Gripping the edges of a sink in the men's bathroom, I stared down at the running water, trying to catch my breath. When I thought I had everything under control, I looked up in the mirror and someone stood behind me.

"Motherfucker," I yelled at Robby. "You scared the shit out of me. Don't stand so creepily behind me, weirdo."

Squirting some soap on my hands, I finished what I'd original came into the bathroom to do in the first place. Robby stepped up to the sink beside me to stare at me some more. I avoided looking in his direction.

"You know," he commented, as if we were suddenly friends and it was okay to have bathroom chit-chat like we were women. "When we were younger, I swear to God, Clara had feelings for you."

I grunted. "Then you were sniffing too much of your mom's perfume. Clara hated me. Hell, I'm pretty sure she had a crush on you back then."

"Just listen," he urged. "When you lost your virginity to Leah Longerburger—"

"Oh my fucking God! Is this coming up again?" With my wet hands, I pulled at my hair, not caring that I was messing it up. "The universe hates me."

Robby grabbed my shoulders with his two large hands, forcing me to look at him. Other men in the bathroom stared at us like we were deranged. We probably were. I would have shoved him off me too, but he was twice as big as me and truthfully, whenever I saw Clara again, I didn't want to have a black eye. Or two. On top of a million other things I was going to have to explain to her.

"Leah was beyond proud of her ability to steal your virtue," he shared. "I hadn't even thought about all this in years—but I remembered this morning when Leah's name was mentioned."

I glared at him. "Do you have a point?"

"Yes," he groaned, dropping his grip from my shoulders. "My point is that when you slept with Leah, the whole country club knew. Hell, I'm pretty sure all of Blue Creek knew. It was juicy gossip and small-towners eat that stuff for breakfast. And I knew you and Clara had some weird relationship going on where you argued all day. A 'fight-mance,' if you will. Which, by the way, grossed me out. It was like foreplay for you two. You made everyone around you want to vomit. Anyway…back to my point here. The same day I heard about you and Leah, I noticed a change in Clara. She must have heard the rumor. And whether she knew she liked you then or not, your big v-card news *hurt* her. Instead of being carefree and easygoing, suddenly she shut down. She became very stoic. And I noticed that the little 'fight-mance' the two of you had going…well, that changed too. It turned downright mean. You screwed up back then, Leo, and I don't even think you realized it at the time. You had her and you ruined it. So, don't ruin it again today."

That shaking, barely breathing thing that I had going on…well, it doubled. No, tripled. "Are you sure about this?" I choked out.

"No. But what if I'm right?"

It killed me thinking that I might have hurt Clara in the past and not even realized it. "All this time—what if I could have been with her all this time and I was too stupid to notice my feelings were reciprocated?"

"Trust me, Leo," Robby said, "I've made a lot of similar mistakes. That's why when you see Clara today, you're going to drop the bullshit. If you care about her as much as I suspect you do then you should just be honest with her. That makes you vulnerable as hell, but if you don't give her everything then…then you're probably going to end up just like your father one day. Alone."

Throwing a nasty look his way, I walked for the exit. I was downright sick of people telling me how I'd turn into my father one day. "Thanks for the advice, *Dan*."

"Anytime, roomie."

Rolling my eyes, we left the bathroom to go join the others. The whole group appeared to be waiting on me. Maggie looked especially concerned. She pulled me aside immediately. "We've got another five hours to go," she whispered. "Calm down, Leo—"

Oh, God. "Jesus Christ. Fuck me," I whispered.

Across the crowded airport, one person caught my eye.

Clara.

I ran. Not even able to help myself or bothering to mention anything to the others, I started to move. She was here…and so I ran.

Just short of closing the final feet between us, I stopped. My knees felt a little wobbly as I stood there before her. It was hard to believe she was actually here. Her blonde hair was extra wild today and her eyes were tired, but I didn't miss the small smile that came to her lips as she took me in. Damn, she was a beautiful sight for sore eyes.

Her suitcase slipped out of her hand, falling to the ground beside her feet. Her big eyes were a force of nature as they stared into mine. We were frozen in place as people swirled around us, all hurrying on to their different destinations.

"Hey," I muttered, both nervousness and excitement bubbling in the pit of my stomach.

Her smile widened. "Hey."

"What's that?" I nodded to the stuffed animal she held in her hands. She squeezed it so roughly, I think its head was about to pop off.

"Um…an armadillo." She stared down at the gray thing. "I got him in the gift shop in Phoenix. It's dumb, I know, but I got him for you."

My heart rate spiked a little. "They have armadillos in Arizona? I thought that was Texas."

Her cheeks flushed and her smile vanished as she shook off my comment. "You're right. It's really stupid." Then she bent down, unzipping her suitcase as fast as she could as if she was about to bury my gift away in her suitcase.

I bent down with her, my hand stopping hers on the zipper of her bag. “Give me the stuffed animal, Clara,” I said softly.

Taking a few deep breaths, she let go of the little guy. In all my life no one had ever given me a stuffed animal before. Actually, for as much as the people in my life traveled, no one had ever brought me home a souvenir at all. I stood, checking out the armadillo. It was cute in an ugly sort of way. And, just because it came from her, it instantly became my favorite possession. Clara stood too, fidgeting and clearly anxious about her gift.

“He reminded me of you,” she explained, “because armadillos have hard shells. But then at the same time, they're cute and soft on the inside. And—”

“You're so fucking adorable,” I uttered, cutting her off. Because she was and I couldn’t resist saying so.

“What?” Her eyes darted up to meet mine.

“You heard me. I love your gift, and I especially love how flustered you're getting. It's really sexy. I have tons of expensive shit and nothing I own means as much as this. It means you thought of me while you were away.” I dug around in my pocket. “I actually got you something too. And now you can watch while I get flustered.” I pulled out my Harry Winston gift. “Give me your hand,” I commanded.

As nervous as I’d been talking in the bathroom with Robby minutes ago, I felt surprisingly calm now. Clara was back in my life. And between her gift, her mysterious phone call yesterday, and the shaky nervous way about her right now—I knew she’d come home just for me. I knew I had her heart. Nothing had ever been so painfully clear to me before. And that made my own heart swell and sing.

She extended her hand. My fingers traced against her skin as I clasped the bracelet—a charm bracelet with only one charm—around her wrist. It wasn't flashy or covered in diamonds. Because I knew Clara wouldn't have wanted something like that. It was simple silver links in various sizes and one four-leaf clover charm.

"Leo?" She glanced from the bracelet up to me. Tears were on the brink of her eyes.

I swallowed hard, feeling all jittery once again. "I can remember that night in my library perfectly. And for years I searched through random books, finding nothing and thinking the clover was lost forever. *Great Expectations*. I had forgotten the title until you said it on the subway. That's the actual clover, by the way. I had it dipped in white gold. I've always wanted to give it back to you. I feel like I've been waiting a lifetime for this."

"Holy shit," she muttered. I couldn't tell if that was a good *holy shit* or a bad one.

Rubbing one hand across my neck, I tried to give her an out just in case she wasn't into it. "I know you never wear jewelry...so if you'd rather wear it as a necklace or something else or not at all, I'll understand."

"No," she gasped, "it's perfect."

"I'm going to say stupid shit sometimes," I blurted out, wanting to talk about us now. "That's a given. And you're probably going to find new and interesting ways to piss me off. That's a given too. But nothing can take away from the fact that I love you, and I'm pretty sure you love me, too. At the end of the day, that's all that will ever matter. I know you're not going to trust me one-hundred percent immediately, given our history, but one day you will. And I know you will because I'm going to spend the rest of my life proving that, yes, I am an ass, but...I'm your ass." I sighed, burying my face in the furry body of the armadillo. "Fuck. That came out awful."

Clara finally closed the distance between us. She pulled my hands down away from my face. "Nope, it was perfect…and so are you. I love flustered Leo just as much as I love the rest of you."

My heart clinched. "Say that again," I demanded.

"What?"

"You know what."

"I love you," she whispered.

It was the single best thing she'd ever said to me—that anyone had ever said to me. And then suddenly Clara jumped up in my arms, gripping my neck tight, squeezing her legs around my waist, and pressing her lips to mine. Not so gracefully either, I might add. My heart was flying in a way it never had before.

"Dammit," I growled into her sexy little mouth. "What is it with you and airports? Do you enjoy trying to make me hard for the whole world to see?" I smiled against her lips. "It's another one of your sweet ways you try to murder me, isn't it, killer?"

"Shut up and kiss me, you ass," she groaned playfully.

And I did. Her lips were warm against mine and her mouth hot as she opened up for me. She made the blood pumping through me feel like fire, just like she did every time we had kissed, and I couldn't get enough. I didn't think I'd ever be able to get enough.

We broke apart only when a girly squeal interrupted us. I set Clara down and a second later Stephany tackled her with a hug.

"Where did you come from?" Clara asked, confused but excited to see her friend.

Stephany hugged her harder. "Sorry, but I had to stop you before you screwed Leo in front of your whole family," she whispered.

A second later, Reed and Maggie, plus a few stragglers, joined us. Any other day I might have cared that they'd all witnessed that kiss. But not today.

"You brought an entourage?" Clara asked Stephany.

"Leo brought an entourage," Stephany corrected.

Clara groaned. "Seriously?"

I pulled at her hand, getting her attention. "I realized—after Maggie found all of the Arizona printouts in your room—that maybe our argument wasn't the only thing that sent you running."

"No, it wasn't," she admitted. "But you're the *only* reason that brought me back. So… this is about to get super awkward."

A second later, the others surrounded her, blocking the flow of traffic through the airport.

"Did you two kiss and make up?" Maggie jokingly asked.

I didn't bother to answer her question and instead reached to pick up Clara's suitcase. As I stood up straight, I whispered against my girl's ear, "Talk to your family, Clara. Instead of pretending like you don't care, just talk to them. They love you and you need to realize that." Then, right in front of Reed and everyone, I pressed a lingering kiss to her lips. As we parted, I said to the rest of the group, "anyone without Ryder DNA...follow me *now*."

And they followed, everyone leaving Clara to talk with her sister and father.

There seemed to be a mutual agreement that some sort of family pow-wow needed to happen. Clara needed to sort some issues out with her family. She needed to know how worried they were and how much they truly loved her. And she needed to do it all without me.

So that was what happened. I lead the others away to some empty seats where we all relaxed and waited. Ten minutes or so ticked by. And by the time we were all leaving the airport, the only thing I felt inside was relief. Immense, soul-cleansing relief.

"Well," Reed said to the group. "Let's move on outta here. We're gonna have a big party tonight at the club for Sinclair's birthday. Not that I need any other reason to celebrate—I've got both my girls right where they belong."

I approached Clara from behind, wrapping an arm over her shoulders and tucking her in close against my side. She fit there perfectly and I never wanted her to leave. While everyone else started moving toward the exit, we fell several steps behind.

"I was right, wasn't I?" I asked. "Your family loves you and there was no fucking way they were going to let you disappear to Arizona."

She rolled her eyes, smiling. "Yeah, yeah. You were right."

"I'm always right, so you should probably get used to it."

She laughed. Then pulling at my arm, to whisper in my ear, "The only thing I plan on getting used to is spending more time with you."

I stopped walking. "When we get back to Blue Creek, you're coming over to my place and we're making up for lost time." My voice went low, turning into more of growl. "I want you naked in my bed with your legs wrapped around me. I've missed having my little snuggler with me this week."

Her eyes widened in shock. "I snuggle?"

"You don't just snuggle, you cling. It's really nice." I pressed a kiss to her temple. "Because as tough as you are most of the time, I like when you show me your softer side."

She stared at me, stunned.

"C'mon, your family is waiting for us," I said, tugging on her hand. The others were yards ahead of us. We caught up and the entire clan left the airport, heading toward where Reed had parked his Range Rover.

After cramming inside and heading straight for the very back seat, Clara curled against my side. We were both beyond exhausted.

"Oh, here's your phone," I said, pulling it from my pocket to hand to her. "I got it from Leah."

"Thanks," she muttered. Whether she knew my history with Leah or not, she didn't mention it. But she did start staring at her phone. "You emailed me? A few days ago?"

"Delete it," I said quietly, so the rest of the car wouldn't hear us. "You don't need to read it."

I'd forgotten about the desperate email I'd sent her when she first went missing. She didn't need to see that.

"Why? Is it mean?" she asked.

"No. It's sappy as shit and irrelevant now that you came home."

"Oh."

Yeah, that seemed to only make Clara want to read it more. She sat there, reading as Reed started the car and started driving back toward Blue Creek. I thought over the words I'd written to her a few days ago.

Once upon a time, there was a skinny little blonde girl, no taller than a tadpole, with a big heart and an even bigger mouth. And then there was the boy next door. He loved her his whole life, but never knew how to handle that. So, he pushed her away and pushed her away, until one night he fell off a railing and bumped his head. She appeared, as if by magic, and picked him up off the ground. She kept an eye on him, even though she should have pushed him away for always being so mean. He knew then that nothing in his life would ever be worth anything until he figured out a way to win her heart...

I stepped in front of the golf cart, Clara. You hitting me wasn't an accident. I saw you coming and I had to do something. Because if I didn't...then one day, I would blink and you'd be gone, happily married with two-point-five kids to some guy who wasn't me. I stepped in front of it...expecting nothing more than a bruised ass, but gaining everything.

And since I'm confessing everything right now, I need you to know that I lied when I said *don't expect me to always chase after you when you pull this kind of bullshit.* I'd chase you a million times and then a million more.

So, I'm coming to find you and when I do, I'm bringing you home. I knew what I wanted when I was six and that hasn't changed…it never will either. Don't even try to argue with me about this one because you'll lose. I love you.

Yours, Leo

She finished reading. I feared for a small moment that my words would frighten her, send her running all over again, but they didn't. Instead Clara snuggled closer into my side. She said nothing and I tightened my grip around her waist.

It was clear to me now.

I'd been the idiot for waiting half a lifetime to tell this girl how I truly felt. There was some merit to the words Robby had spoken to me in the bathroom. The emotion that rolled off Clara in this moment told me everything I needed to know. Even if she hadn't known the way I'd always known, she loved me now. And always. This was the way it was supposed to be.

And she'd always belonged with me.

CHAPTER 21:

Parting ways sucked some serious balls. By the time we drove home from the airport, stopped at McDonalds, and made it back to my house, it was late afternoon. And, trust me, McDonalds had *not* been my call. The only thought rolling around in my head all afternoon was getting Clara home, getting her alone, and then getting her undressed. Food was more like an afterthought. Especially fast food. I wasn't even a fast food kind of a person. So by the time we finally reached my house, I was antsy as hell and slightly sick to my stomach.

And then Reed dropped me off at my front porch. Alone.

"Bye, Leo," he said, smiling and hanging his head out of his driver side window of his Escalade. He waved his fingers at me. "We'll see you later tonight. I know how you need your space and your time to get ready."

My mouth dropped open a little. "Okay then." *Was he dismissing me?* I was a little confused.

Sure, my appearance was important to me and I knew I took longer than the average male to get ready. Okay, maybe even longer than the average female too. But I wasn't as much of a diva as he was insinuating. To make this moment worse, I kind of expected Clara to hop out of the car and follow me inside, but she didn't. I guess it was too awkward and inappropriate having her father unload us both in front of my empty house.

Because the sexual tension between Clara and I had been thick all afternoon. Maybe Reed could sense it too and was trying to do the fatherly thing. Who the hell knows?

So I unlocked my front door and went into my house. Alone. Robby had mentioned something about taking Valerie back to his apartment to start packing his belongings—or something like that. I wasn't really paying attention, so I can't be certain. Not that I cared much either way. But they didn't get out of the car either. So it was just me.

Marching up the staircase, I hurried for my room. I figured I could shower and head back over to Clara's house. There were still a few more hours left before the party started. And time with Clara—supervised or unsupervised—was better than none.

I stripped out of my clothes, leaving them in a pile on my bathroom floor. Then I started the water in my shower. The water had just moved past freezing cold when I heard a small knock.

Turning quickly, I opened the door. And there was Clara—slightly out of breath and staring at me. Her eyes took in my naked body. And, *fuck me*, did they like to linger. My whole body started to buzz and the blood in my veins pumped a little harder. The fact that I was already naked and the sound of my shower running behind me only magnified everything.

"Um, hey, Jesus." She blew out a breath and her eyes flickered up to meet mine. "I got as far as the end of your driveway before I realized that I didn't care if that whole carload of people knew going with you into your house meant we were about to have sex. So I jumped out of the car and ran up your driveway. And then up your steps. This house is entirely too big and I don't think—"

I silenced her words with a kiss.

Not a gentle one either, I might add, because I couldn't even pretend to wait another second longer. I needed her. Now. We had lost time to make up for. Hell, lost *years* to make up for. And she was right. Worrying about what other people thought wasn't what I wanted either of us to waste our time on.

So without hesitation, I gripped the edges of Clara's shirt and lifted it over her head. I dropped her shirt to the floor as she kicked off her shoes. Then we worked quickly together to rid her of the rest of her clothes. We were both breathing a little too heavy by the time I finished. Reaching behind her, I used my palm to press the door closed. Nobody was home, but I felt more comfortable shutting out the rest of the world.

After that, I dropped to my knees. So much relief coursed through me. Like a giant bolder had been rolled off my chest. Having her here, alone in my house, tucked away with me, made my mind feel so blissfully at ease.

Moving over her bare stomach, I pressed little kisses along her skin as I went. Her fingers weaved through my hair. Then with my hands, I gently nudged her legs apart. Just slightly. She complied and moved for me. I needed only a little space. And I thought I could keep my shit together as I did this, but seeing her step apart for me, while I was kneeling before her at eye level, had me ready to combust.

"Damn, Clara," I muttered.

Unable to stop myself, I pressed a wet kiss against her. She sighed as my lips made contact, while her fingers in my hair fisted and tugged slightly.

"I missed you," she whispered. Her voice cracked with emotion, making me pause right then and there next to her. "I know this is new, but I missed you so damn much while I was away. Moving to Arizona is something I've wanted for years—because I thought it would fill some missing piece inside me. But I got to Arizona and instead of enjoying it, I only thought of you. You're my Arizona."

I stood to my feet, cupping her face with my hands. "Clara, when did your feelings for me start?"

"I don't know." She took a few deep breaths, staring straight into my eyes. "I don't know. That's the crazy thing. I honestly don't know."

I didn't need her to pinpoint an exact date. We were together now and that was the only thing that mattered. But I could hear it in her voice and see it in her eyes. I hadn't spent a lifetime alone in my feelings. A piece of her had always felt something for me. That was for damn certain.

"Shower?" I asked, breathing in deeply through my nose.

She nodded.

Bending, I gripped her bare thighs and lifted. Her legs locked around my waist automatically, her breasts pressing nicely against my chest. Then I carried her into the shower. The water had grown hot and steam filled the bathroom. My shower was big enough for five people, beautiful stone from floor to ceiling, and I pressed her back against the far side wall beside one of the shower heads. Water ran down over our joined bodies.

And we kissed.

I loved the way the sensation of her mouth was quickly becoming familiar to me.

Then I adjusted, standing on the balls of my feet, bringing the head of my cock up to her entrance, and slowly I pushed inside her. She gasped as her body stretched for me. "Are we going to do this standing up?" she whispered, incredulous.

Hell, yes.

I nodded. Then gripped her more firmly under her thighs, easing myself out and then back in. I repeated this rhythm, over and over. Fucking her easy and lazy at first, but then my movements soon grew powerful and fast. I had a lot to teach this girl, the girl I planned to make my wife one day, and shower sex was only the beginning.

She held on tight as I continued, my vision and my thoughts blurring.

And then suddenly she was coming. Her cries filled the shower and her fingernails dug into the muscles of my shoulders. "Leo," she screamed. "Oh, God. Yes!"

That was my undoing. Pleasure exploded in a wave over my whole body. I came harder than I ever had before. Tremor after wonderful tremor rocked me. Dropping my head to her shoulder, I let out a cry. This moment and this girl—they were better than anything on earth money could buy. I'd always hoped for that to be true and now I knew with absolute certainty that it was true.

I got the girl I'd always wanted.

THE END

And now…

A preview of the alternative version to Leo Maddox…

HE BELONGS WITH ME

SARAH DARLINGTON

PROLOGUE

CLARA

My dad, the one and only Reed Ryder, had been golfing professionally for the last quarter century. As a younger man, Dad was the shit. Golf's golden boy. Insanely good looking. All-American. Dad's likeability factor propelled his celebrity status to legendary overnight. Riding the waves of his new success and fame, he met my Mom—a Southern beauty with golden curls and an unbreakable spirit. The two fell madly in love, were married, and had perfect twin baby girls. Wanting a retreat for his new family that was out of the media spotlight, Dad built a beautiful house and a country club in the southern Virginia town of Blue Creek.

Talk about a golfer's wet dream. The Reed Ryder Country Club, located in the middle of nowhere, was like no other. With the help of his best friend—Leonardo Maddox the second, heir to the Maddox Hotel fortune—Dad spent millions designing and perfecting the ultimate golf getaway. Word quickly spread about the lush 'little slice of heaven' nestled in the Blue Ridge Mountains and soon others wanted in. Mr. Maddox built a luxurious hotel to accommodate the numerous vacationers and even more of the wealthy flocked in, which resulted in grand vacation homes popping up all over Blue Creek. So that's how the Reed Ryder Country Club came into existence, and how the once quiet town of Blue Creek, Virginia made its mark on the map.

The golfer, the beautiful wife, the twin girls, the best friend and his family, the country club in the mountains…this is our story.

And oh yeah, for the record, he most definitely belongs with *me.*

CHAPTER 1

MAGGIE

Desperation kept me from falling as I stumbled across the gravel parking lot in my red, Jimmy Choo, sky-high stilettos. God help me. I was about to enter the grungiest, ugliest, most run-down bar in the city—Mike's Pub. I'd driven past this place countless times but never dared go inside.

Until now.

My mission—my one care in the world at this moment—was to find a guy named Dean. My plan was to ask him to be my date. Tonight, the Reed Ryder Country Club was hosting its official gala to kick off the summer season and who better to accompany me than a total stranger, right? Judging by the bar I was about to enter, Dean was better off staying a stranger. Nevertheless, that's why he'd be perfect for this evening.

The goal tonight: shock and awe. A new rumor involving me, one that was unfortunately true, would begin to circulate soon, and maybe if I created a rumor of my own I could trump the first. My plan was juvenile, but it was all I had. I'd been to three other bars looking for this guy. If I couldn't find him here, then I'd be forced to head to the dance dateless. He *had* to be here.

As I approached the front door of Mike's, several middle-aged men—cigarettes and beers in hand—stared open-mouthed at me. I drew attention in my crimson-red Zac Posen dress, the lush material clinging to my petite body like a second skin. The dress had a long slit up one leg that would make Jennifer Lopez proud. To top off my elegant look, I'd worn my naturally platinum-blonde hair parted far to one side, circa 1920s. My hair had natural wave to it, but I'd straightened and then re-curled it in big waves to ensure that the style was just right. And it was perfect, though I hardly looked my age or appropriate for such a dive bar.

Keeping my head held high, I passed several men concealed by clouds of smoke and pushed my way through the heavy double doors into the unknown. Gulping down any remaining fear, I dared my first glance around at my surroundings. If I'd thought the outside was bad, the inside was worse…much worse. The rotting floorboards reeked of urine and mold, and the clientele wasn't much better—beer bellies and mullets were in plentiful supply. I was pretty positive all horror films started in places like this.

The infamous Dean—apparently some sort of walking sex on a stick—couldn't possibly be any of these strangers. I was beginning to think he was more fairytale than real life anyway, and therefore my brilliant idea to ask him to be my date took a nosedive straight into the trash. Settling for someone else wasn't an option either. If I wanted to shock and awe, then I couldn't arrive with Mr. Shockingly Awful. Going to the gala dateless, as pathetic as that would be, seemed like my only choice.

Accepting defeat, I headed back toward the door when a woman with the body of a flagpole approached me. She wore a tight-fitted white t-shirt, a server's apron, and a plastered-on smile. Her eyes took in my dress with envy. "Ain't you a fancy one? Ya lookin' fer someone?" Like any local in town, her voice carried a strong Appalachian dialect. Thankfully, my speech carried no trace of that distinctly southern Virginia twang, even though I had to try my best to hide it sometimes.

"Do you, by chance, know a guy named Dean? I'm not sure what his last name is."

Realization dawned on her face. "I shoulda guessed you'd be here fer him." The bony woman whipped around and, in no particular direction, yelled, "Dean! I found ya 'nother stray!" before facing me again. "He's workin' at the bar. Good luck, sugar. You'll need it."

The server's slightly back-handed comments might have bothered me on a regular day, but not under the current circumstances and not with the clock ticking against me. The dance started fifteen minutes ago and this would be my only shot at a date. I sure hoped this Dean guy was everything Anita said he would be. He just *had* to be.

I got my first glimpse of the man working behind the counter and knew he was the one I'd been searching for. *Hello, Mr. Hottie-Boom-Body.* Early twenties, wickedly handsome, and totally worth the nightmare I'd suffered through to find him—*thank you, Anita.* But it wasn't just his pretty face that made him the perfect choice, it was his size. Between his height, width, and all the muscle in between, his size demanded attention. If I could show up with him tonight, then everyone on the gala guest list would notice. He was everything shock and awe had to offer. Now I just needed to convince him to be my date.

I walked confidently toward him like his looks weren't overwhelming. His light honey-colored, almost golden eyes locked with mine. Despite the low lighting, they stood out against his ruffled, brown hair. There was a sexy warmth about him that reminded me of something I couldn't quite put my finger on. Whatever it was, it made him the perfect choice for tonight. Not quite what I'd been expecting—better.

"You must be Dean," I said, finally face-to-face with the guy I'd spent the last two hours trying to hunt down. Well, face-to-chest. He stood well over a foot taller than me, and up close, the intimidation factor was almost too much to bear. Behind the counter, his big hands worked quickly as they expertly mixed different drinks. I couldn't help but think about what *else* he could do with those hands. At that thought, I tried to remind myself that my motivations tonight were strictly business. A slight smile formed on his lips and it helped me regain some confidence.

"You *are* Dean, right?"

The corners of his mouth reached wider into an even more charming smile. Did I amuse him or was the dress working its magic? He leaned over the bar to get a better look at me, and I tried not to feel flustered as he gave me the once-over.

"Who's asking?" His voice was gruff and completely void of any accent. *Interesting.*

"My name's Maggie Ryder."

"As in Reed Ryder, the golf pro?"

"Yes, Reed is my dad."

"Well then, what can I do for you, Maggie Ryder?"

There was no easy way to say what I came here to say, so I just blurted it out. "I know this is going to sound insane, but I need a date. There's a big party at my dad's golf club tonight and I absolutely, positively cannot show up alone. I need you. I need you to be my date. And I need this to happen like ten minutes ago."

He chuckled and handed a mixed drink to a customer down the bar. When he returned, he looked as if he was waiting for me to say, "Gotcha," but this was no joking matter. I waited for his response, and when it became clear I wasn't messing around, the easy smile left his face.

"That's an odd request. Why me?"

I twirled a curl of my hair between two fingers—something I often did when under scrutiny—and tried to keep an even face. "I want something...um, *someone* different. Look, my reasons are kind of personal and I don't feel like getting into the details. I understand it's a lot to ask on such short notice, but I'm kind of desperate. Can you help me or not?"

"You're a pretty girl. I'm sure you've got the boys lined up. Besides, as you can see," he said, indicating the dirty dive bar with a wave of one of his strong arms, "I'm kind of working."

My eyes were having trouble leaving those arms. He certainly wasn't a boy and I certainly wasn't after a boy. "I could pay you for your time. A couple hours, that's all I'm asking. Can you find someone to cover your shift? I'll wait if I have to."

His jaw tightened, telling me his answer was 'no.'

"Pretty please."

"I can't," he stated, his voice firm and unwavering. "I'm not an escort service."

Shame rose to my cheeks. He was right. I hadn't realized the insanity of my request until now. Did I really think I could pay a stranger to be my date? My life wasn't an eighties movie and this sure as heck wasn't *Can't Buy Me Love.* This guy had morals. Where were mine? Maybe it was because of his good looks, but I suddenly felt all the embarrassment I should have earlier.

"You're right, I'm sorry. I shouldn't have wasted your time."

I turned tail and hurried for the exit, past all the lingering eyes, and back into the cool night air. *Stupid. Stupid. Stupid.* As fast as my Jimmy Choos would allow, I raced to my Porsche 911, aka Baby, desperate to put Mike's Pub and Dean in my rearview mirror. But it wasn't my outlandish idea that bothered me so much, it was how quick Dean had turned me down. I'd known the guy for all of five seconds and somehow he'd gotten to me.

Digging for my keys with shaky hands, I dropped my purse and its contents onto the gravel. *Dang it!* I bent over to gather my things, put my purse back in order, and when I made it back on my feet, a cry of shock left my lips—Dean.

Taking no notice of the heart attack he'd just given me, he crossed his arms over his broad chest and said, “I could trade a favor for a favor.” Gone was the apprehension I'd seen moments ago and instead, amusement lingered on his lips. Was he bipolar or something? “Money turns me into a slut. A favor, that's different.”

“What? You'll do it?” I asked, though inwardly wondering if I even still *wanted* him as my date. This guy just took confusing to a whole new level.

“That's what I just said.”

I cocked an eyebrow at him. “What kind of favor?”

He shrugged. “One to be redeemed at a later date.”

“What exactly does *that* mean?”

“It means I don't know what I want right this moment. Nothing sexual or illegal, of course.” He cocked *his* eyebrow at me. “But maybe later I'll want something in return. Does that sound fair to you?”

I stared up at his face and tried to decipher his motives. He wasn't just some backwoods country bumpkin. He was smart—smarter than his bartending job might lead one to believe. I could tell that much from the moment he first opened his mouth.

“You want me to cash you a blank check?”

“When you put it that way, you make me sound like some sleazy politician. But yes, I want a blank check. Those are my terms.”

“Nothing sexual or illegal, right?”

As he nodded, I realized that I was fine with the whole favor-for-a-favor thing, and I certainly wouldn’t complain if I had to see him again in the future. So at this point, we were just wasting time.

“Deal.” I jutted out my hand out for him to shake. “One favor to be redeemed at a later date."

"Deal," he said, taking my hand in his. "Pleasure doing business with you, Miss Maggie Ryder."

AN HOUR HAD PASSED since I made my agreement with Dean and I'd spent every minute of it waiting. Waiting for him to find a replacement to cover his shift at the bar. Waiting for him to make a random phone call—probably to a girlfriend or something. Waiting for him to shower and change into some decent clothes. After what seemed like forever, he finally came out of his apartment and got in my car.

"You're worse than a girl," I mumbled, shifting into gear and pulling away from his rundown apartment complex. *Who knew hiring a date would be so much work?* Trying to make up for the lost time, I drove my car like I stole it, pressing heavily on the gas and zipping down the empty streets. We were so late, I wasn't even sure if it was still worth going.

"Beauty takes time," he said smugly. "Besides, you didn't want me going in my smelly clothes from the bar. And you've got to admit, I do clean up rather nicely."

He looked so cramped in the small space of the Porsche that I couldn't help but smile. And he was right; he did clean up well. Maybe even a little *too* well. He now wore a black suit, white dress shirt, and a black tie. All of it non-designer. All of it simple. But I doubted anything ever looked simple on this guy. He could make a paper bag look good, but the suit was more appropriate for the occasion.

The fresh scent of soap and mint filled the air between us, causing me to momentarily forget everything else. I caught myself sneaking glimpses of him out of the corner of my eye and urged said eye to stay on the road. Fortunately, a potentially embarrassing situation was interrupted by a voice belonging to the object of my not-so-stealthy observations.

"Out of curiosity, who should I be thanking for the pleasure of your company tonight?"

I'd been waiting for him to ask this question. It sure took him a while to get around to it. "My friend Anita, who is also the manager at the club's restaurant. She told me about you."

"I don't know an Anita. Should I?"

"She didn't she say she knew you personally. She just knew *of* you. Or had seen you around town…or something to that effect." I flipped the gear stick down into second as I rounded a tight corner. We'd be at Dad's country club in less than a minute. My nerves started to creep in on me now that we were getting so close. Would tonight be a horrific failure or a brilliant success? Everything hinged on the stranger seated next to me.

"What all did this Anita person tell you?"

"Not much. Just that you were handsome, wild, a local, and that people would notice you. I can't remember the exact details."

He chuckled low to himself. "Wild? Interesting description. Are you hoping for a taste of my wild side, Maggie?"

"We're here," I announced, completely avoiding his question.

The car jolted to a stop as we pulled into the valet parking zone, and a wave of nausea hit me like a punch to the stomach. I'd been wrapped up in the conversation with Dean, but now that we were here, all I could think about was my impending doom.

"Oh God, I don't know if I can do this," I thought aloud.

"You can," he said, his voice sounding kind. "Trust me, you'll be fine."

I didn't know him well enough to trust him. And he'd only just met me so I'm not sure why he seemed so convinced I could do this. Going inside meant I'd be facing Andrew Wellington—my ex—and a major reason as to why I'd gone searching for Dean in the first place. I dated Andrew my senior year of high school and throughout the past three years of college.

We did the long-distance thing, which seemed to work for us, and I figured we'd be together forever. Then he dumped me last semester and I learned that our whole relationship had been nothing more than a colossal waste of time. He'd be here tonight.

But the icing on the cake was Clara—his brand new girlfriend. Her betrayal hurt more than anything Andrew could have ever put me through, and she was the real reason I needed a person like Dean at my side. I think I'd be fine never seeing Andrew again, but I had to prove to everyone that Clara couldn't hurt me. More importantly, I had to prove to Clara that she couldn't hurt me.

"Maggie?" Dean asked. I guess I must have zoned out there for a moment. "Did you hear me, Maggie? Are you okay?"

I gulped, watching as the valet guy—Kevin—came hurrying toward my car. "Yeah, peaches," I muttered without thinking, "just peaches."

"Peaches? Don't you mean 'peachy' instead?"

I didn't answer him but jumped out of the car, followed by Dean. Without hesitation, I handed over my keys to Kevin and gave him a quick hug. He was one of Dad's loyal employees and I'd known him for years. Kevin drove my car away and I hurried for the door. Ready or not—this was it.

"Wait." One strong hand wrapped around my arm, forcing my determined stride to a halt.

"We're already late, Dean." My voice came out rather shaky. "Can't it wait until we're inside?" I squirmed, trying to shake off his grip, but it was no use. Dean had a firm hold on me and wasn't letting go.

"Look at me, please," he demanded.

"No. Let. Go."

"Sorry, but not until you look at me first."

I twisted and turned, but he still wouldn't budge. What was his problem? Now heated, I glared up at him. At five foot nothing, I had to crook my neck just to get a good look at his face, and I was surprised to find that something protective shown in his eyes.

"You should take a breath," he said in a soft voice. "Calm down for a moment. You're so distracted that you're blind to what's right in front of you. I don't know who your boyfriend is, what the bastard did to hurt you, or why you thought I'd be the solution to all your problems, but you need to calm down before you go inside." His words were sincere, hardly expected from a big guy like him.

"Ex," I corrected.

"Who cares? A woman in a red dress came into my bar tonight, and never in my life had I seen someone with so much confidence or command over a room. Where is that woman now? Get it together, Maggie. I know you're stronger than this."

He stood over me, unmoving, while his relentless eyes continued to hold my gaze. I took in a couple of deep breaths, trying to decide if I should be flattered or angry by his comments. Never before had I been spoken to like that—at least not by a stranger. His honesty was brutal and I finally landed on angry.

"I'm fine," I assured him through gritted teeth. "You can let go now. And don't ask any more questions because I'm done answering them. Peaches?"

"I still don't understand what that means."

"It means let go of my arm—please."

I yanked away and this time, he let me break free without a fight. It had been a mistake bringing him. A big one, I decided. I couldn't believe Dean had the audacity to grab me in public like that. No one had seen us—everyone was inside—but still. I rushed for the door, planning to leave him outside, but he kept close as if nothing strange had just happened, walking inside with me.

“Since you're still determined to be my date, there's one last thing you need to know,” I whispered to him as we entered. “My ex, Andrew Wellington, will be here tonight with his new girlfriend. Oh, and just a head’s up…his new girlfriend is my twin.”

CHAPTER 2

CLARA

I hated grass. Loathed it. And everything it represented.

With his sweaty fingers laced through mine, Andrew Wellington led me down the fairway of the sixteenth hole. If Dad knew I was out here at night—trespassing and trudging all over his precious golf course in my stilettos—he'd shit a brick. Maybe even a whole house. I didn't care. I dug my heels harder into the grass. Except with my luck, I was probably only helping to aerate the damn stuff.

The only comforting thought at the moment was that one day I'd move someplace far, far away—Arizona, specifically—where the yards were made of pebbles instead of sickeningly perfect grass. I'd leave everything behind and never come back. I didn't necessarily want to cut ties with my family, just everything else that came with being a Ryder. I already had an escape plan in the works, and I knew that it was only a matter of time before I worked up the courage to actually carry it out.

"It's beautiful out here at night, isn't it?" my sister's ex-boyfriend asked. My identical twin's ex-boyfriend of four years, to be exact. Whom I was currently dating. Or pretending to date.

He released my hand from its damp captivity and strolled a few paces ahead of me. He stood and gazed around like a total weirdo, a huge unexplained smile on his lips. It was only a golf course, for goodness' sake—not freaking Disney World. Maybe I would admit, and only if someone twisted my arm, that most normal people might agree with Andrew. The crickets chirped. The stars twinkled. The overhead spotlights illuminated the course in a way that regular sunlight just couldn't. And something about the stillness amplified everything. Except, I just couldn't see the beauty that I knew was smack-dab in front of my face. Or even if I could see, I damn well couldn't appreciate it.

Summer break officially started ten days ago. I'd successfully finished my junior year at Virginia Tech, and while most of my friends were off tackling their first internships, doing the horizontal tango with someone special, taking fabulous family vacations, or simply hanging behind in Blacksburg so they wouldn't miss all the summer parties, I was being held hostage here in the dreadful town of Blue Creek. Secluded, quaint, and nestled along the Blue Ridge Mountains. Population: pitiful. Historical significance: zip. Suicide rate: *extremely* likely. At least I could take comfort in the fact that this would be my final summer under Dad's thumb. Oh, and best of all, it was the last time I'd be stuck working at his stupid, uppity country club.

I'd been home from college all of one day before Andrew asked me out. Naturally, I declined. As my sister's ex, the guy was strictly off-limits. It didn't matter that Maggie and I weren't exactly best buds. Hell, these days we were barely on speaking terms. But I wasn't a bitch. No matter what my relationship with my sister looked like, I wouldn't stoop that low.

Still, Andrew had been annoyingly persistent. It felt nice being pursued like that, since guys typically steered clear of me. They preferred the nicer, sweeter version of myself—Maggie. But for some mysterious reason, Andrew kept at it. I'd been almost tempted (*not!*) until I discovered from my friend, Leah Longerburger that persistence and charm were just part of the Andrew Wellington playbook. Apparently, he got around and not just recently. When I found out the slime-bucket had been cheating on my sister—with Leah and multiple others—*that's* when I finally agreed to go out with him.

Come hell or high water, my mission this summer was to make Andrew Wellington regret he ever knew the name Clara Ryder. When Andrew confessed that he had feelings for me—that he'd always had feelings for me—my first thought had been absolute disgust. How could he have dated Maggie for all those years and carried some secret torch for me? But as he made his declaration of love, I hadn't missed the sincerity behind his eyes. That's when I formulated my plan to fake-date him. He'd crushed Maggie's heart and now I was going to crush his. Payback was going to be a bitch.

But in addition to hurting Andrew, I also had to protect Maggie. My biggest fear was that after I crushed and dumped Andrew, he'd go running straight back to my sister. What if she took him back? My sister let people into her heart so easily, and since she dated the dillweed for four years, I got the impression that she might still be hung up on him. My relationship with Maggie was already broken, no matter what I did. So, my great-big-awesome plan not only consisted of breaking his heart, but also giving Maggie the impression that her "perfect" Andrew was vile enough to bang her sister. Not exactly honorable, but in my deranged mind I saw the plan as brilliance.

Maybe it would've been easier to just tell her the truth, but I doubted she'd have believed me. I needed insurance and my plan offered that. Plus, it gave me something to do this summer. Blue Creek was dreadfully boring. A little scandal sounded fun.

"Andrew," I whispered in my best seductive voice. "We're all alone and you're more interested in the golf course than the beautiful girl standing right beside you. I didn't come all the way out here to admire the grass."

A smile formed on his smug lips, and then he suddenly closed the distance between us. His hands tangled through my long hair. His mouth smothered mine. His dry lips needed some serious ChapStick, but I kissed him back like I wasn't repulsed. When his slobbery tongue plunged into my mouth, I very nearly vomited, but somehow I managed to keep it together. We'd kissed twice now but never so greedily. Was he trying to eat my face?

He shimmied out of his suit jacket and glued his body to mine as his hands traveled downward. Then, to my surprise, he yanked me up in his arms, and the next thing I knew he was lowering me down onto the prickly grass I hated so much. His consuming kisses didn't stop there and neither did his hands. He pushed his way between my legs, inching up my dress, and I felt his rather puny erection pressing against me. Can you say awkward? The only thing separating my 'V' from his 'P' was a couple layers of clothing. *Holy shitballs!* This wasn't what I had in mind when I'd suggested we take a walk instead of going to the party. I had to stop this before I lost my V-card to the last person I ever wanted touching me.

"Andrew," I breathed against his mouth, giving his chest a small nudge, "it's too fast."

Putting on the brakes, he wasted zero time shoving his body off mine but took no care in covering the giant sigh that escaped his lips as he plopped down in the grass beside me. Staying still for a moment, I tried to collect my thoughts. I wanted to give Maggie the impression that I'd screwed him—not *actually* screw him. What if Andrew wouldn't have stopped just now? A jolt of fear shot through me. I normally would have never put myself in such a vulnerable position, and the close call made me want to get the hell back to a more populated area…now.

"We should go to the party. My dad is expecting me there."

"No problem." Hardly rattled, he sat up and reached for his jacket. While his attention was elsewhere, a glorious light bulb popped into my head. Lots of people liked to get freaky out on the golf course at night, so I plucked a handful of grass and rubbed into my hair. Maggie never missed a single party at the club, and hopefully when she saw it, she would assume I'd been getting hot and heavy out here. Maybe *that* would help boost her hatred for the skuz-wad.

Andrew stood to his feet, noticing nothing, and then helped me up.

"I'm sorry. I didn't mean to spoil the moment. I just... I just..." I trailed off, fumbling all over my fake apology. Fake or real, I wasn't sure what the appropriate words were for this type of situation. We began walking back across the fairway toward the distant lights of the clubhouse. Talk about awkward. I tried to come up with something—anything—to say, while ignoring the blades of grass that kept falling from my head. "I'm sorry," I mumbled.

"I know," Andrew said, his words earnest and soft. "I know you're not a slut. I told you before, I've always noticed you. You don't have to explain yourself. We'll get to the good stuff when we get to the good stuff. I would never rush you."

For a fraction of a moment, I almost believed the toolbox was a halfway decent guy. Maybe I even saw what my sister had always seen in him. Then the disturbing image of Andrew getting freaky with Leah Longerburger sprang into my head, and I lost my respect for him all over again.

About the Author:

Sarah Darlington lives in Virginia with her husband and son. She's a former flight attendant, navy brat, constant day-dreamer, wannabe photographer, and an avid scrapbooker. She loves to travel and is working on visiting all 50 states.

Books by Sarah Darlington:

He Belongs with Me

Leo Maddox

Kill Devil Hills Series:

Kill Devil Hills

Changing Tides

Coming Summer 2015: ***Pulled Under***

Coming 2016: ***Adrift***

Made in the USA
Middletown, DE
12 May 2015